What was ha

Sure, Tessa was
sure, the valley n
Tessa lived in the States, for heaven's sake! She had nothing to do with him. She was here for maybe a week.

Which was all very sensible, Mike thought, but logic didn't account for the way his heart lurched when he saw her.

Marion Lennox has had a variety of careers—medical receptionist, computer programmer and teacher. Married, with two young children, she now lives in rural Victoria, Australia. Her wish for an occupation which would allow her to remain at home with her children, her dogs, the cat and the budgie led her to attempt writing a novel.

Recent titles by the same author:

THE BABY AFFAIR
HIJACKED HONEYMOON
DR McIVER'S BABY

BACHELOR CURE

BY
MARION LENNOX

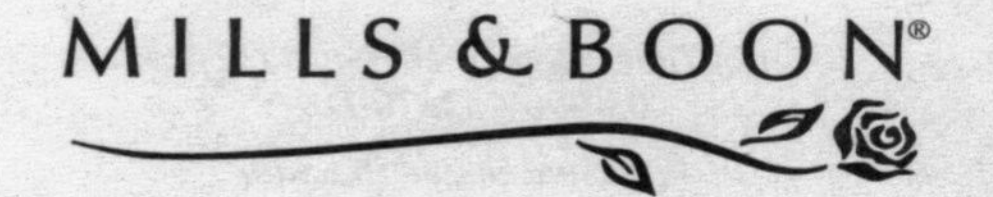

First published in Great Britain 1999
Harlequin Mills & Boon Limited,
Eton House, 18-24 Paradise Road, Richmond, Surrey TW9 1SR

ISBN 0 263 81792 X

Set in Times Roman 10½ on 11½ pt.
03-9909-53670-D

Printed and bound in Spain
by Litografia Rosés S.A., Barcelona

PROLOGUE

MIKE LLEWELLYN pushed the dark curls out of his eyes and looked wildly around him. The mountains where he lived had always seemed his friends and, heaven knew, he stood in need of friends now. His bony shoulders trembled, and his hands clenched into fists of helplessness.

Sixteen years old was too young an age to face this. The doctor was here now, but Mike knew in his heart that it was too late.

Over and over, the doctor's words played in his mind.

'You should have called me sooner, you stupid boy. Don't you realize your mother's dying?'

Yes, he did know, and the accusation was unfair. He'd phoned over and over again, but the doctor's wife hadn't helped a bit.

'He's out. That's all I know. Don't ask me where he is. He's just out.'

After scores of frantic phone calls, the whole district had started searching, but the locals knew what the doctor would be doing. He'd be somewhere with a woman who wasn't his wife, and he'd probably be drunk. The valley's only doctor would have no intention of being found.

In the end the doctor had arrived back at the surgery full of drunken bluster, saying he'd had his radio on all the time and no one had called him.

Liar!

'The man's a liar,' Mike said to the mountains, and tears of frustration and rage welled behind his eyes. He blinked them back but others came fast to replace them.

And at that moment he made himself a silent vow. It was

a promise he made to nothing but the mountains, but it was a vow he intended to keep for the rest of his life.

'I'll be a doctor myself,' he swore. 'I'll be the best doctor I can make myself and I'll come back here and work. And that's all I'm going to do. No woman's ever going to interfere with my work. There's no way anyone else in this place will die like this—not if I can help it. No matter what happens now…'

And then he turned to face what was happening inside. He turned to face the emptiness of his future.

CHAPTER ONE

THERE was a girl in red stilettos lying in Henry Westcott's barn. Or rather, she was lying under Henry Westcott's pig.

Mike had met the police car at the gate. 'There's someone mucking around at Henry's place,' the sergeant had told him curtly. 'Jacob saw the light from his place. Want to back us up—give us a bit more manpower?'

He didn't. Jacob Jeffries was a rifle-toting bonehead, and the thought of making a posse with him was enough to make Mike queasy. Still, Sergeant Morris was the only policeman in the district and he'd helped Mike out of tight spots in the past. Checking deserted farmhouses for thieves was risky, and Jacob might look tough but, given any real danger, he'd run a mile.

So he'd come, leaving Strop guarding his precious Aston Martin. But now...

Mike stopped dead as the police sergeant threw open the barn door and flooded the place with light. They'd been expecting petty thieves, or maybe even Henry himself, but they certainly hadn't been expecting this.

The girl was lying flat in the straw, her arm immersed to the elbow in pig. She was young—in her twenties, from the look of her—slightly built and fiery.

Fiery?

Yes. Definitely fiery. She was practically all scarlet. The girl was wearing a tiny, tight-fitting, crimson skirt. The slim legs stretched out behind her on the straw were clad in clear stockings with a crimson seam, and her feet were clad in red stilettos. She was wearing a white blouse, but her flaming curls were tumbling about her shoulders and hiding most of it so he could mostly see just legs and redness.

Mike couldn't see her face. Her face was pressed into the straw and the rest of her was hidden by pig. What on earth…?

'OK. You're covered. Stand up slow, then raise your hands over your shoulders.' Unlike Mike and Sergeant Morris, Jacob knew exactly what to do. He'd seen it on the telly. He'd been expecting criminals and Jacob didn't change his mind fast. 'Be careful,' the sergeant had told him before he'd flung open the door. 'Whoever's inside could be armed.' So Jacob was in threat mode.

'Don't even think about producing a gun,' he barked, waving his rifle in the direction of the pig and the wonderful red stilettos. 'Throw down any weapons.'

'Jacob,' Mike said faintly. 'Shut up.'

He was the first to move. The girl had been using a kerosene lamp to see by, but Sergeant Morris had a heavy searchlight which was now flooding the barn with light. The sergeant stood, shocked into stillness. Jacob waved his gun while he tried to figure things out, and Mike walked forward to see what was happening.

The girl's face was turned away from him on the straw. He stepped over her and crouched so he could see more.

She had a great face. She had gorgeous clear skin, and big green eyes, and a slash of crimson lipstick the exact shade of those ridiculous shoes…

Her face was contorted in agony.

The girl had a bucket of soapy water beside her which told its own story. He winced in sympathy. Ouch! He knew what that was for.

Mike had come out here tonight because Henry Westcott was missing, believed dead. He knew how fond Henry Westcott was of his pig, and checking on Doris was something he could do for an old man he was fond of. He'd visited Doris the day before, and he knew her time was near.

So the piglets were on their way—sort of. He winced again. Lifting the bucket, he poured soapy water gently over the girl's elbow as she penetrated the birth canal.

The girl gave a grunt of what might have been called gratitude. Her arm came out an inch or so to get some more lubrication and she went straight back in. The pig's body heaved and the girl gave a sob of pain.

Hell!

He didn't need to be told what was happening here. The pig's belly was so swollen, there had to be more than half a dozen piglets trying to get out. But now… Something was clearly obstructing the birth canal. The girl was trying to clear it and it was no wonder she looked like she was in pain. Every time the sow had a contraction, massive muscles would be squeezing this girl's arm with power beyond endurance.

'I said stand up,' Jacob barked behind them, but he was ignored. The police sergeant sighed and lifted Jacob's rifle so it wasn't pointing downwards, but the girl didn't care. She was only intent on one thing. The pig.

Mike could only admire her singlemindedness.

Once, when he'd been a junior resident in a large teaching hospital, he'd been watching open heart surgery when the fire alarm had sounded and the smell of smoke had wafted through Theatre. The hospital staff had reacted in well-ordered panic, but the surgeon had kept right on operating.

'Forget the alarm,' he'd growled. 'You can have any fire you like, but not until I have this closed!'

That determination was what he saw again in this girl's face. She was in pain and Jacob's threats must have got through to her, but she was concentrating on one thing and one thing only—clearing the birth canal.

There was nothing he could do to help. There certainly wasn't room in the birth canal for two of them.

'Talk me through it,' he said urgently, his face almost touching the girl's. 'What's going wrong?'

'There's a piglet stuck...'

She had a voice to match her face. It was exhausted and pain-filled, but it was soft and lilting and...gorgeous!

'You can feel it?'

A contraction hit. Doris's body strained in a massive movement of muscle and the girl's body jerked sideways.

'You can't do this,' he said savagely, and he put his hands on her shoulders to try and draw her out. Hell, she'd break every bone in her arm.

'No. No! I can feel a hoof. Leave me!'

She shoved herself further forward. 'More water,' she gasped. He splashed a bit more water over her arm and then took the bar of soap and ran it around the vaginal entrance. If he had time... He had lubricants in the car...

'I have it,' she whispered. 'One. Two. Three... Don't muck me up now. I have four hooves. Please, Doris, hold the contractions... I have to push...'

'What the...?'

'There're four hooves coming down at once and the head's right back,' she muttered into the pig, and he didn't know if she was talking to him or to herself. 'It's stuck like a cork. I need to get it up. I need to push...'

Another contraction. It jerked Tessa's arm, hauling her body with it.

She was so slight!

She had to be slight to succeed. No man could get his arm into that canal. Cows maybe, but not pigs.

'Bring the light over,' Mike ordered, his eyes not leaving the girl's face. There was agony written there, but also sheer, bloody-minded determination. 'Jacob, go and get my bag from the car.'

'But what's happening?' It was taking Jacob a long time to work out he was in on a birth, rather than taking part in a criminal raid. He sounded totally bewildered.

'We're having piglets,' Mike said into the stillness. 'At least I hope we are.'

His hands came down and held the girl's shoulders, gripping hard, letting her move as she willed but giving her support when she needed it so the pig's contractions stopped jerking her sideways.

He was trying to let her feel she wasn't alone. It was all he could do, and it wasn't enough. He felt utterly helpless in the face of her pain.

Who on earth was she?

He could feel the effort she was making. Once each contraction had passed, she put everything she had into shoving the piglet forward, upward and higher. During the contraction she concentrated on holding it back and not letting her efforts be wasted. He could feel her whole body straining.

She must know some obstetrics. The only way to get the piglet out if it was firmly wedged was to push it back and turn it.

Was she a vet—*in those stilettos*?

And then he felt the piglet give—a minuscule amount but he felt the girl's body jerk forward and she gave a gasp of sheer relief.

'Turn, damn you. Turn,' she muttered, as her own body changed position. 'Please…'

Her shoulder twisted and her face screwed up. The crimson lipstick looked almost surrealistic.

And then her shoulder twisted still more. She gave a grunt of surprise and pain. The sow's body contracted in one huge mass of muscle and the girl's arm came sliding out.

Her hand was grasping one dead piglet.

The piglet slid limply onto the straw. The girl shoved it

away as if it was of no importance—as indeed it wasn't—and then she shoved her hand into the soapy water and moved again to reinsert it.

It wasn't needed.

The contraction didn't ease. It became a rolling crescendo of muscle power, and another piglet slid out onto the straw. This one was alive.

It was followed by another.

It was as if a cork had been pulled from a champagne bottle. Doris's exhausted body heaved with every ounce of energy she had left, and minutes later the girl was in the middle of a squirming, bloody mass of living piglets.

Five. Six. Seven. Eight live piglets.

Mike was so stunned he could hardly count, but Doris knew. As the last of the piglets was expelled from her body, the massive sow moved her head around to see what she'd finally produced.

The girl looked up into the sow's face and grinned—heavens, what a grin! She tried to lift one of the piglets around to its mother.

Her arm didn't work. She gave a whimper of pain and the piglet fell back onto the straw.

Mike gave her a long, searching look and then he took over. At least he could help with this. He lifted each of the piglets in turn to lie under its mother's eye.

After three piglets, the police sergeant finally came to his senses. He'd been watching in stunned silence, playing the floodlight over the birth. Now he set his searchlight down on a bale of hay and started ferrying piglets.

Which left Mike to concentrate on the girl.

She was exhausted.

No longer needed, she wilted. She lay back on the hay and clutched her arm as if it might fall off. Her face was dead white, her lipstick was smeared and there was the glimmer of tears in those gorgeous eyes.

Jacob came pelting back into the barn with Mike's bag and the crazy gun still waving.

'I've got it. I've got it,' he told them, and skidded to a halt inches from Mike. Mike put a hand up and took the gun—followed by the bag.

'That's great, Jacob,' he said calmly. He lifted the dead piglet and put it into the big farmer's hands. 'Now, go and bury this before Doris figures it's alive and starts protecting it.'

'Why the hell…?' Jacob stared down at the battered little body lying in his hands. 'We still don't know what she's doing here and you want me to bury this? Why?'

'Because it's dead, Jacob.'

'Oh. Yeah.' Jacob stared down at the body in his hands. 'Right.' He looked over at the policeman. 'You don't need me any more? For her, I mean?'

'I think we can handle this,' the sergeant told him dryly. Then, as Jacob moved to take his rifle back from Mike, the policeman shook his head. 'No, Jacob. Leave the gun here. It's not needed.'

'But…' Jacob was clearly uneasy about giving up his crook-chasing role. He cast an uncertain glance at the girl. 'We don't know who she is. She could be anyone. We dunno.'

'No,' the sergeant said. 'But I think we can assume she's not here to steal anything. And if she runs…' He grinned. 'I reckon we can catch her in those heels.'

The sergeant was right. The girl wasn't going anywhere.

As Jacob carted the unfortunate piglet towards the door, the girl pushed herself up to a sitting position and gazed about her. She put a bloodied hand up to push back her curls, and left a gory streak down the side of her face.

She looked young and crazily vulnerable.

She looked hurt.

She'd only used one arm to push herself up. Now she

brought her good arm over and cradled the other arm against her breast.

'Let me see,' Mike said gently, crouching before her and putting a tentative hand on her arm. She winced and pulled back, and the look of pain in her face deepened.

'No. I need... I need...'

'She must be on drugs,' Jacob interrupted knowledgeably, pausing before he walked out the door with the dead piglet. He still wanted the criminal element here. He'd come expecting crooks and he was determined to find some. 'I'll bet that's what she's up to here, Sarge. You can't tell me normal women wear shoes like this. She'll be on drugs.'

'Drugs!' The pain from her shoulder jabbed again like a hot poker. Mike could see it in her face. The girl was bloodied, filthy and hurting, and she was so exhausted she could hardly speak. She looked exposed and humiliated. And now...

Now, suddenly, her overwhelming emotion was anger. Mike watched it running through her, supplanting the pain. She hauled herself to her feet. With her good arm, she shoved her skirt down in a futile attempt at dignity, and she glared at Mike and the policeman for all she was worth. Five feet six of flaming virago facing two unknown males! She wasn't scared, though, Mike saw. She was too plain angry to be scared, and...she really was beautiful!

'Who are you?' he asked mildly, and that was the last straw.

'Who am I? *Who are you?*' she demanded. 'Who the hell are *you*? You're on my grandfather's property. What gives *you* the right to demand to know who *I* am? To talk about drugs? What gives you the right to come here with guns?'

And then, suddenly, it was all too much. The girl's shoulder had jerked as she'd pulled herself upright. He could see in her eyes that the pain was indescribably fierce. So fierce she couldn't bear it.

She gasped and staggered, and she would have fallen, but Mike was right there, holding her tightly by her good arm, stopping her from falling and propelling her down onto one of the tumbled bales of hay.

'It's OK.' His voice, when he spoke, was as gentle as the laughter lines around his eyes. It was deep, resonant and sure, and, as always, it was inexplicably reassuring. The locals said his forte was small children and dogs, and they had reason. Mike's was a voice that imbued trust. 'Don't fight it,' he said softly. 'It's OK.'

The girl didn't lack courage. She did resist—she pulled back for all of two seconds—but if she didn't sit she'd fall, and there was no choice. She sat, and looked helplessly up again at him as she tried to clear the mists of pain. You could see what she was thinking.

Who the *hell* was this?

'It's OK,' he repeated again, and there was such gentleness in his tone that it made the girl catch her breath. 'We're not here to hurt you.'

'Where…where's my grandfather?'

'We've been searching for him.' He knelt before her, and his fingers gripped hers, blood and all. His hands were big and strong and warm, and they clasped hers as if he knew how scared she was underneath the bravado. It was a gesture of warmth and strength and reassurance he'd used many times before, and the girl's body relaxed just a smidgen. Nothing more, but he could feel it, and he smiled his reassuring smile—a smile that could charm a rattlesnake.

'I'm the local doctor,' he told her. 'Let me see your arm. Let me help.'

'It's nothing.'

He ignored her protest. The girl was in no condition to talk coherently, much less think. He watched her face—his eyes asked permission and his hands moved to the top button of her blouse. 'Can I see?' Then, as she didn't object, he undid her soft cotton collar and pulled the cloth away from her shoulder. He whistled soundlessly. No wonder she looked as if she was in pain.

'You've dislocated your shoulder.'

'Just leave it.'

The girl's words were a pain-filled whisper. Courage was oozing out of her as reaction set in.

'You're not to be frightened,' he told her, taking her hands again but so gently he didn't jar her injured arm. 'We're here to help, and there's nothing to be frightened of. I'm Mike Llewellyn, Bellanor's only doctor. Behind me is Sergeant Ted Morris and Jacob—the chap who's burying the pig—is your grandfather's neighbour. He owns the farm next door. We've been searching for your grandfather since he went missing four days ago.'

'But…' The girl looked as if she was desperately trying to make some sense of what he was saying. She wasn't succeeding. All she could think of was the pain.

'Explanations can wait,' Mike said firmly. He took the wrist of her injured arm and carefully lifted it so her arm was in a sling position. 'I can take you back to the surgery and manipulate this with anaesthetic, but if you trust me then I can probably get your shoulder back into position now. It will hurt, but so will travelling over rough roads to get you to town. I can give you some morphine, but I think the best thing to do is just manipulate it back in fast. Will you try to relax and see what I can do?'

'You…you really are a doctor?'

'I really am a doctor.' He smiled down at her, his blue eyes gentle and reassuring. He was hauling on his best bedside manner and then some. 'The sergeant here will tell you. I even have a certificate somewhere to prove it.'

'And…you know how to get this back?'

'I've put back dislocated shoulders before.'

The girl looked up, her eyes doubtful. This wasn't the normal person's idea of a doctor. He wasn't wearing white coat and stethoscope. He wore blue jeans and a rough wool sweater. He had deep black hair that curled in an unruly tangle and needed a cut, and his face was tanned and his eyes were crinkled, as if he spent a lot of time outdoors.

He wasn't the least bit doctor-like.

But he had piercing blue eyes, and a smile on his broad, tanned face that told her she could put herself safely in his hands. It was his very best bedside manner, turned on in force, and it usually worked a treat.

Now was no exception. The girl sighed and nodded, closed her eyes and forced herself to go limp. She waited, waited for the pain…

He looked down at her in surprise. Had this happened to her before, then? She looked like she knew what to expect.

There was no point dragging it out.

He lifted her wrist, bent her elbow to slightly higher than ninety degrees, then slowly, firmly, rotated her arm down and back—so firmly that the girl gave a sob of agony.

And then, miraculously, it was over. The shoulder clicked right back into place.

Silence.

The girl took two deep breaths. Three. Four. And then she opened her eyes to a pain-free world.

Her green eyes crinkled into a smile of absolute relief. 'Thank you.'

The girl's words said it all. There was no need for him to check his handiwork. The girl's breathed words of gratitude and the easing of the agony behind her eyes told him all he needed to know. He smiled down at her, and she smiled right back—and it was some smile!

'Well done.' He put a hand on her good shoulder.

Tessa's courage was amazing. 'Brave girl. Don't move yet. Take your time. There's no rush.'

No rush...

Her smile faded and the girl looked about her in bewilderment, as if seeing where she was for the first time. Doris lay exhausted on the straw. Around the sow, the piglets were starting their first, tentative movements toward her teats.

Someone had to break the silence, and it was finally the police sergeant who did.

'Now, young lady, suppose you tell us just who—'

The policeman's voice was gruff, but Mike put a hand on his arm, shook his head at him and silenced him with a hard look.

'Nope. Questions can wait, Ted. She's done in. She's Henry's granddaughter. That's all we need to know.'

'You're the girl who phoned from the US earlier this week?' the policeman asked.

'Yes. I...I'm Tessa Westcott. I flew in this afternoon, hired a car and came straight here.'

'We don't need to know any more,' Mike said firmly, and Tessa's eyes flew to his face.

What she saw there seemed to reassure her. Mike's was a face of strength—strongly boned, with wide mouth, firm chin and lean, sculpted lines. There were traces of fatigue around his deep blue eyes, but his eyes sent strong messages of kindness and caring. He ran a hand up through his dark tousled hair, his eyes smiled at her and the impression of reassurance deepened.

'If Henry Westcott's your grandfather, how come we've never heard of you?' The barking demand came from behind, and Mike wheeled in sudden anger. It was Jacob, who'd come back into the barn to find a shovel.

'Jacob, lay off. Can't you see we've scared the girl stupid? She's hurt and she's frightened and now's not the time to start a full-scale interrogation.'

The radio on the police sergeant's belt crackled into life. The sergeant lifted it and talked briefly and then he sighed.

'I have to go,' he told them as he replaced it. 'The Murchisons' cows have got out again and they're all over the road near the river bend. If I don't get down there soon, someone's going to hit one.' He looked closely at Tess. 'I knew that Henry had a grandkid in the US, though, and you sure have his hair. We need to talk, but maybe...'

'Not now,' Mike told him. 'Tessa, you're past talking.' He stared down at the girl before him, his quick mind figuring out what to do for the best here. 'Sergeant, could you use the radio to ask the vet to come out here and see Doris? She'll need antibiotics straight away and I don't have a clue as to dosage. If Jacob stays here to help, he should be able to treat her. If Tessa doesn't mind sharing my passenger seat with Strop, I'll take her into town.'

Strop... Tess shook her head, confused. 'I'm staying here,' she said.

'I don't blame you.' The policeman grinned. 'You wait till you meet Strop. Sharing a passenger seat, indeed...'

'There's nothing wrong with Strop that a good vacuum cleaner can't fix,' Mike said with dignity. 'Strop is my dog, Tess, and he'll be very pleased to meet you.' He hesitated as her look of confusion increased. This girl was in no fit state to be making decisions. She could barely hear him, and she certainly wasn't fit to spend the night alone in a deserted farmhouse. 'You'll spend tonight in hospital and let me have a good look at that arm,' he said firmly. 'You can come back tomorrow, if you're up to it.'

'Doc, are you saying I have to stay here?' Jacob demanded incredulously. 'Are you saying you expect me to stay with the pig and wait for the vet?'

'After scaring Miss Westcott stupid, it's the least you

can do,' he said blandly. 'And I know you, Jacob. You always do the least you can do. Besides, in the last year I've made five house calls to your place in the middle of the night for your sick kids, and every one of them could have waited until morning. Call this payment of a debt.'

Jacob shook his head, confused, and to her amazement Tess felt herself start to smile. She'd blinked at Mike's curt orders, but she needn't have worried. Jacob wasn't the least bit offended. He thought Mike's words through and then nodded, acknowledging their fairness.

'We need to go now,' Mike told Tess, only the faintest trace of humour behind his deep eyes telling Tess that he was also laughing gently. 'I have a patient in labour myself. She was in the early stages when I left and she isn't likely to deliver until morning, but she needs me all the same. OK, Tess?'

She looked as if she was operating in a daze. Nothing seemed to make sense. 'I…' She was forcing herself to focus. 'I guess.'

'That's fine, then.' He smiled down at her. 'I'm sure Jacob and the vet will take the greatest care of Doris. Bill Rodick, the vet, is very competent, and Jacob's a fine farmer. So… You can visit Doris tomorrow if she's up to receiving callers. Now, though… Strop makes a great chaperon. That's his principal mission in life—to obstruct as many things as possible. So do you trust Strop and me enough to let us drive you to town?'

Trust him?

Tess looked up, and she gave Mike a shaky smile—and then, before she could realise what he intended, she was swept up into a pair of strong, muscled arms and held close against his rough sweater. She gasped.

'No. Please… I can walk..'

'I dare say you can,' he told her firmly. This girl had enough courage for anything. 'But it's dark outside. I know where my car is. I'm sure-footed as a cat and I don't want you stumbling with that arm, especially if Strop's abandoned his leather armchair and is back at his old trick of obstructing things. He's the type of dog burglars fear most because they're at risk of tripping over him in the dark. So shut up and be carried, Miss Westcott.'

Shut up and be carried...

It seemed there was nothing else to be done—so Tess shut up and was carried.

Mike carried the girl out to his car and tried to figure just what it was about her that made him feel strange.

Like he was on the edge of a precipice.

CHAPTER TWO

THE girl was quite lovely.

The clock on the wall said three o'clock, and Tessa's hospital bed was bathed in afternoon sunlight. Mike had stuck his head around the door three or four times during the morning but each time Tess was still sleeping soundly. Now she opened her eyes as he entered, blinked twice and tried to smile.

Tess was in a single hospital ward, small and comfortably furnished, with windows looking out over a garden to rolling pasture beyond. It was cattle country, if she had the energy to look.

She didn't. She stared across at Mike as if she was trying to work out just who he was.

This was a different Mike to the one she'd seen the night before. He'd told her he was a doctor and, after his treatment of her shoulder, Tess had had no grounds for disbelief. But now… In clean clothes, his black curls brushed until they were almost ordered, a white coat over his tailored trousers and a stethoscope swinging from his pocket, he was every inch the medico.

He still had the bedside manner she remembered from the night before. He stood at the door and smiled, and Tess was forced to smile back.

And then her gaze dropped in astonishment. A vast liver and white basset-hound was sauntering into her room beside him.

'Awake at last?' Mike's lazy smile deepened as he strolled over to her bed, trying not to appreciate her loveliness too much as he did. The fact that the look of her almost took his breath away didn't make for a placid doctor-patient relationship at all. 'Welcome to the land of the living, Miss Westcott.' His eyes were warm and twinkling. 'How's the shoulder?'

'It seems fine.' She kept on staring at Strop. 'So there really was a dog,' she said. 'I thought he was part of my nightmare.'

'What, Strop?' Mike grinned. 'He's no nightmare. He's solidly grounded in reality. So well grounded, in fact, that if he gets any closer to the ground we'll have to fit him with wheels.'

'You keep a dog in the hospital?'

'He's a hospital dog. He has qualifications in toilet training, symptom sharing and sympathy. Just try him.'

Strop looked up toward the bed. His vast, mournful eyes met Tessa's, limpid in their melancholy. He gave a faint wag of his tail, but went straight back to being mournful.

'Oh, I can see that.' Tess chuckled. 'He'd make any patient feel better immediately. Like they're not the only ones feeling awful, and they couldn't possibly be feeling as awful as that!'

Strop flopped himself wearily down on the bedside mat. Mike shoved him gently aside with his foot—the dog slid under the bed without a protest as if this was what happened all the time—and then Mike turned his attention back to his patient.

That wasn't hard to do.

'Enough,' he said. 'Strop steals my limelight all the time. Your arm, Miss Westcott. How is it?'

Tess wriggled it experimentally and winced. 'I wouldn't worry about it. It's bruised but it's fine. You must have put the humerus right back in or it'd hurt a lot more than this.'

'The humerus…' Mike's face stilled. Last night he'd suspected she had obstetric knowledge, and now… 'You're a nurse, then?'

'Nope.' She smiled and it was like a blaze of sunshine. 'Guess again.'

'A physio? An osteopath?'

'Try doctor.'

'A doctor!' He stared.

'Females can be,' she said, still smiling. Her voice was gently teasing. 'In the States, medicine's about fifty-fifty. Don't tell me you still keep women in their place down under.'

'No. But…' Mike thought back to the crazy red stilettos. He stared down, and there they were, parked neatly side by side under the bed beside Strop. Crimson stilettos. And… A doctor?

'And doctors are allowed to wear whatever they like,' she told him, following his gaze and knowing what he was thinking in a flash. 'There's no need for us to put on black lace-ups when we graduate—so you can take that slapped-by-a-wet-fish look off your face, Dr Llewellyn. Right now.'

'No. Right.' He took a deep breath and managed a smile. 'You're a practising doctor, then?'

'That's right. I work in Emergency in LA.'

'Yeah?'

'Yeah.'

'Well, that's put me on my mettle.' He had himself back in hand now. Almost. 'Doctors are the worst patients,' he said, and tried a grin. 'They're almost as scary to treat as lawyers.' He sat on the bed beside her and tried to ignore the weird feel of intimacy his action created. Hell, he sat on all his patients beds! 'Your shoulder's really OK?'

Tess moved it cautiously against the pillows and winced again.

'It's sore,' she admitted. 'But it's definitely back in position. It's just bruised.'

'Can I see?'

'Sure.' There was no reason why he shouldn't. There was

no reason why she should blush either as he loosened her hospital gown and gently examined the shoulder and the bruising of her arm. He was just a doctor, after all…

His fingers were gentle and sure, and his eyes watched her face as he carefully tested the injured arm. 'Do you have full movement?'

'I can wiggle everything,' she told him. 'But I don't want to.'

He smiled. 'I don't blame you. In a day or two it'll look really spectacular.' He ran his hands over the bruised arm, trying to block out his thoughts of Tessa the woman and turn them back to Tessa the patient. Usually he had no problem with differentiating work from personalities, but Tessa was something else! And her blush didn't help at all.

'You may not want to wiggle, but you'll live,' he pronounced finally. He pulled the sheet back to cover her and tucked her in.

It was a caring gesture that he made every day of his working life but suddenly the gesture was far, far different. Intimate. He stood looking down at the girl in the bed, struggling to maintain his lazy smile.

'You might even feel like living after your sleep,' he said finally, shoving away the strange sensations he was feeling and striving hard to sound normal. His smile deepened. 'Fifteen hours' straight sleep isn't bad.'

'I don't think I've slept since I knew Grandpa was missing,' she admitted. She grimaced. 'And to sleep fifteen hours now, when I should be out searching for Grandpa…'

'There's no need for you to be out searching, Tess. The police and the locals are all looking as hard as they can, and they're being thorough.'

'I know the farm, though. I know the places he loved to go.'

'But—'

'But what?' She glared up at him. 'What? Why do you sound like that?'

'Like what?'

'Like you're trying to scotch any ideas I might have of where he might be.'

He sighed. This was hard. Bloody hard. But, then, telling families the worst was something he'd had to face many times.

'Tess, your grandfather has mitral valve disease and atrial fibrillation,' he said softly. 'He's been missing for over four days now. It's my guess... Well, that farm of his is as rugged as any around here. There're plenty of places a body could lie for months and not be found. Your grandfather is eighty-three years old. If he went out and had a heart attack...well, my guess is that's exactly what's happened. His truck's still at the house. He had his goats tethered and Doris due to deliver. If he was going away, he'd have organised people to care for them.'

'I know that,' Tess said. She stared up, and any trace of her gorgeous smile had completely disappeared. Her distress was obvious. 'But... I didn't know he had heart disease.'

'Have you been in contact with him recently?' he asked. 'I was under the impression he had no contact with his family.'

'He and my dad didn't get along,' she said bleakly. She was obviously still taking the heart disease bit on board and was thinking it through as she talked. She turned and stared out the window, fighting to get her face back in order, and it was as if she was talking to herself. 'Dad and Grandpa fought. Dad went to the States when he was twenty. He met my mom there and he stayed. He died when I was sixteen, without ever coming back here.'

'I'm sorry.'

'No. Don't be. My family history has nothing to do with

you.' She sighed again and shrugged, turning back to face him. 'Dad was always against me coming back, but he was pig-headed and…well, he was stubborn enough to make me wonder whether the disagreement had all been one way. So when Dad died…Mom said I should know my background so she sent me out to stay. I spent a summer vacation here with Grandpa. I stayed here for three months, just after high school.'

Three months. When Tess was sixteen…

He must have been away at medical school then, he thought. Otherwise he'd surely remember this girl.

'Since then we've kept in touch,' Tess said. 'I write often, so does he, and now I ring him every Saturday. We seem to be getting closer the older he's getting. It's like he's finally acknowledging he needs family. Anyway, when I didn't get an answer this week, no matter how many times I rang, I contacted the police and was told he was missing. So I came.'

So she came. She came halfway across the world to check on her grandfather. That was some commitment.

'But…I didn't know he had heart disease,' she said slowly. 'You would have thought he'd tell me. How bad is it?'

'I guess he hasn't wanted to worry you. He's been taking digoxin and is fairly much under control, but if he was over-exerting himself with no tablets, and if he got too far away from the house…' He hesitated but there was no way to gloss over the truth or make it any easier. 'His pulse rate's been up around a hundred and twenty or so, and without digoxin or even aspirin…'

He didn't continue. He didn't need to.

Tessa's heart wrenched within her, and he saw the pain. His hand came up to touch her lightly on her cheek.

'Don't, Tess,' he said softly. 'I'm hoping that your grandfather's heart just quietly gave out and the end was fast. That's what he would have wanted, to die in the bush he loved.'

'Yes, but…'

But… But they didn't know. They didn't know he had died quickly. The alternative was unspoken between them—the thought of the old man lying helpless in the bush and dying a slow and lingering death.

'Sergeant Morris and a heap of the locals have scoured the farm,' he told her. 'I've been out there, too. We've been everywhere we can think of and we've found nothing. We've called, Tess. If your grandfather was alive then he could have called back. He could be somewhere we've overlooked, but surely he'd be within earshot.'

'Not if he's had a stroke. Not if he can't make his voice work.' Her voice broke off and she choked in distress. 'Mike, I need to look. I need to search myself. There are places… One special place…'

'Yeah? Is this somewhere the police would have found?'

She shook her head. 'I thought of it all the way here. Grandpa showed it to me when I was here as a teenager, and he talked as if it was a really special privilege for me to know about it. It was his secret. It's a cave…'

'In the hills?'

'Yes. I remember it as being just past the boundary of the farm, where the hills start turning rugged. I can't remember much more. In fact, I can't even remember which direction it was. There was no way I could tell the police about it on the phone. And when I got to the farm last night I thought how stupid it was to come all this way on a hunch. Things have changed and my memory's playing tricks on me. Maybe…maybe I can never find it or maybe it's accessible now and someone's already looked. But that's why I came. I want to check. Just as my own contribution to the search.'

She sighed and turned to stare sadly out the window. 'I

know my dad and Grandpa disagreed, but Grandpa sort of saw things in the same way I do.' Then she managed a fleeting grin as she turned back to face him. 'Me and my dad fought, too.'

'Don't tell me. Your dad had red hair as well?'

'And a temper to match. My dad could say some pretty unforgivable things. And Grandpa was...is...a redhead, too.'

'I see.' But he didn't see at all. He stared down at this amazing woman in confusion. She'd come from the other side of the world to search for a grandfather who was probably dead. She had a good job in the States. Had it been OK—just to walk away?

'Hey, my mom's behind me in this,' Tess said quickly. 'She always felt bad about my dad never coming home. She's paid half my airfare.'

'Bully for your mom.' He hesitated, thinking things through, and he raked his fingers thought his thick hair in thought. Tess had come so far, and she needed to conduct her own personal search, but he hated the thought of her scouring that bushland alone. The locals reckoned they'd searched every inch of the farm. Tess would be on her own now.

For her to be alone was unthinkable! And even if she found her grandfather alone...well, that was more unthinkable.

Finally he nodded, flicking through his mental diary at speed. OK. He and Strop could do it.

'Tess, I need to do a couple of hours' work right now,' he told her. 'Have a meal and rest for a bit. Ted's brought your car in. It's parked in the hospital car park and your gear's being brought inside as soon as the orderly has a spare minute. So get yourself into some sensible clothes.' He eyed the stilettoes with caution. 'And some sensible shoes. I'll be back in two hours, and after that I'll come out to the farm with you.'

'You don't have to come with me,' she started, but he stopped her with an upraised hand.

He had work piled a mountain high in front of him, and he was dead tired—the labour he'd looked after last night had been long and difficult and he'd managed all of two hours' sleep—but the thought of Tess searching by herself for what he feared she'd find was unbearable.

'I want to, Tess,' he told her. 'So let me.'

He clicked his fingers. Strop heaved one end up after the other and lumbered to his side, and they left.

Which was just as well. If he'd stayed in that room for one minute longer, with that look on her face—half scared, half forlorn and as courageous as hell—he would have gathered her in his arms and hugged her.

And where was the professional detachment in that?

'I should have refused his offer of help,' Tess told Bill Fetson two minutes later. The hospital's charge nurse had come to check on her and had found her pacing in front of the window. 'Mike was up half the night with me and Doris, and didn't he say he had a baby to deliver after he brought me in? What's he doing, offering to spend hours tonight searching for someone he's sure is dead?'

'He cares about your grandfather.'

'I guess...'

Her voice sounded totally confused, Bill thought, as though there was something about Mike she didn't understand in the least. Well, maybe that was understandable. Mike was a fabulous-looking doctor, with a smile that could turn any girl's head, a dog that was just plain crazy and a presence that played havoc with Bill's nursing staff.

But this girl was different. Bill watched the emotion

playing over her face and strange ideas started forming in the back of his mind. Well, well, well…

'Would you like a tour of the hospital?' he asked mildly—innocently. He was busy, but something told him it might be important to get to know this girl…

Tess showered and dressed, then explored the little hospital. It had fifteen beds, eight of them nursing beds and seven acute. It was a tiny bush nursing hospital, efficient, scrupulously clean and obviously beautifully run. It was almost new, and the man who introduced himself as Charge Nurse showed Tess around with pleasure.

'It's all thanks to Dr Mike,' Bill Fetson said with obvious pride, as he showed Tess though a tiny operating theatre with facilities that her made blink. These facilities would be more in place in a big city teaching hospital. 'Mike fought the politicians every legal way—and a few illegal too, I'll bet—to get this place, and he practically bullied the community into fundraising. Now we have this hospital, though, well, there's no way we're losing it. The valley's never had a medical service like this.'

'How long's he been here?' Tess asked.

'Three years, but in a sense he's been here much longer. Mike's a valley kid and he started fighting for this before he even finished his medical training.'

'And…' There were so many things she didn't understand here. 'He's always had Strop?'

Bill grinned. 'Strop was an accident. Mike drives an Aston Martin—the sleekest car in the valley. The salesman brought it up here for a test drive and drove it too fast, putting it through its paces. Strop was lumbering across a road on a blind bend and the salesman couldn't stop. Mike felt dreadful, and then the woman who owned him said he was a stupid dog anyway and seeing Mike had hit him then Mike could put him down. As you know, the Aston Martin only has two seats. The salesman drove to the vet's with

Mike carrying Strop, and by the time they reached the vet's there was no way he was being put down. So in one afternoon Mike got the sleekest car and the dopiest dog in Christendom.'

'You're kidding.'

'No way. And, believe it or not, he is a great dog.' Bill's grin deepened. 'The patients love him and all the valley knows now that if Mike pays a house call then so does Strop.' He paused, and his smile faded. 'But what about you? I gather you're practically a valley girl yourself. I'm not local myself, but Mike says you're Henry Westcott's granddaughter. And he also says you're a doctor…'

His eyes asked all sorts of questions, but he didn't voice them. Not yet.

Finally, his tour at an end, Bill showed her into a gleaming little kitchen, introduced her to Mrs Thompson, the hospital cook, and left her to be fed. A meal was no trouble, Tess was assured. No trouble at all.

She certainly needed it. Tess ate Mrs Thompson's meat pie with potato chips and lashings of salad. She washed everything down with two huge tumblers of milk and she hardly felt the meal touch sides. Thinking back, she couldn't remember when she'd last had a meal. Maybe she'd fiddled with something on the plane, but how long ago was that? Too long, her stomach said.

Replete for the moment, Tess tentatively broached the idea of she and Mike taking food out to the farm with them. With the size of this hospital, a sole doctor must be run off his legs, and she was starting to feel really guilty about dragging him away.

She needn't have worried about the reaction of the cook. Mrs Thompson practically beamed.

'That's a really good idea,' the middle-aged lady told her, hauling a picnic basket out of a top cupboard. 'Doc Llewellyn hardly stops to eat, and he'll miss dinner entirely if you don't bully him into it. Either that or he'll eat six pieces of toast and three eggs at midnight, which is his usual way. No, dear. I'll pack you a meal fit to feed six of you, including dog food for that misbegotten hound of his, if you promise to see he eats it.'

'He works too hard?' Tess asked cautiously, and the woman nodded with vigour.

'Driven—that's what our Dr Mike is,' she said. 'There's demons driving him, that one. He'll end up in an early grave, mark my words.' Then her look softened. 'But you've more to be worrying over than our Dr Mike. Oh, child, I'm so sorry about your grandfather. I just hope…' She sniffed vigorously. 'I just hope the end was quick!'

'Thank you,' Tess said weakly. She didn't know what else to say.

While her picnic was being prepared, she retreated to her bedroom. She needed the privacy. The hospital was abuzz with who she was, and every nurse and patient in the place was burning with the need to know more. Like…did she have any ideas where her grandpa was?

And there was so little she could tell them.

Mike collected her an hour later.

He walked into her room and stopped in stunned amazement at the transformation. He'd seen Tessa bloody and exhausted and in pain. He hadn't see her like this.

Tess was certainly a beauty in anyone's book. He'd thought so last night and he'd thought it when he'd seen her asleep in her hospital gown. In fact, he thought it every time he looked at her.

She wasn't a classical beauty, but she was a beauty none the less. She was slim and neat and her legs stretched on for ever. In her figure-hugging jeans, she seemed all legs.

Or all eyes, depending on which end you looked at, he thought. Tessa's face had the pale, creamy complexion of a redhead and she'd come straight from the end of a United States winter. There was a faint spread of faded freckles over her nose—echoes of last summer. Tessa's mouth was rosebud-shaped, her nose pertly snub and her face almost all eyes, the greenness framed by her red-gold hair.

She was thin. Well, maybe not too thin, he thought to himself. She was just…just well packaged. She was thin where it counted and not thin where it counted more! In her figure-hugging jeans and close-cut T-shirt, her figure was revealed to perfection. She had an old windcheater draped around her waist, and the trainers on her feet were nearly as old as the clothes he'd changed into, but the age and the casualness of her clothes didn't detract from her beauty one bit.

It was all he could do not to whistle.

He didn't, though. He paused for one millisecond—and then caught himself, smiled and picked up the picnic basket.

'Provisions, Dr Westcott? Hasn't the hospital fed you?'

'Mrs Thompson has personally insisted I eat enough to feed a small army,' she assured him. 'But I wouldn't be the least surprised if I feel the need to eat again quite soon. Even my toes seem hollow.'

He grinned. 'No anorexia, then? Excellent. I like a girl with a healthy appetite.'

'Do you want a cure for anorexia?' she demanded. 'I've just invented it. Put a girl on a plane for thirty-six hours with airline food for company and fear in her stomach, and then toss her among pregnant pigs and dislocate her shoulder. Then put her to sleep for fifteen hours and—hey, presto—you've a girl with a healthy appetite. Magic, Dr Llewellyn! I think I'll write it up as a new wonder treatment for one of our prestigious medical journals.'

'You'll make your name as a medical whizkid,' he told her.

'I know,' she agreed, and fluttered her eyelids in assumed modesty.

Whew! Good grief! He smiled at her, and Tess chuckled—and when Tess Westcott smiled, his body started to heat from his trainers up.

'OK, then, Tess,' he told her finally, and only a faint hesitation under his words hinted at what he was feeling. 'You're fed and rested. Are you ready to face the farm?'

Tess nodded. 'I'm ready.'

'OK. Strop's waiting in the car. Let's go.'

She set her face, and Mike saw grimness replace the laughter behind her eyes. Hell, she had courage. She knew what could lie ahead of them.

This was some woman!

And suddenly he wasn't the least sure he was ready to spend any time with her. There was something deep inside that was telling him he should run a mile.

But there was something else that was telling him to stay.

The farm was dreadful. Even Strop, having made the first half of the trip straddling the gearstick and the second half where he really wanted to be—sitting high on Tessa's lap with his ears flapping out the window—seemed depressed by the place. His mournful ears flopped lower and his eyes welled with moisture. Good grief, you just had to look at the dog and you'd burst into tears! He lumbered off to sniff in the bracken and Tess was pleased to see him go. She was depressed enough without him.

They made a courtesy call on Doris first. She was too preoccupied with her eight babies to notice human visitors. Jacob had done his job well. Mike had rung him early this morning and asked him to make sure the sow was fed and watered, and there was nothing more she needed. Now she had everything she could want, except maybe a spare set of teats.

After paying their social call on Doris, they tackled the house.

There was nothing here to help them—no clues as to where Henry could be. The place was deserted, but it still held the signs of an occupant who hadn't intended to leave. There was milk curdling in the refrigerator. Someone had taken a heap of sausages from the freezer and left them by the stove to defrost. That had been four or five days ago and they were starting to stink.

They cleared up in silence and Mike thought he was glad he hadn't let Tess face this alone. It was only bad sausages, but there were so many dreadful thoughts crowding in, and the smell of rotting meat didn't help one bit.

'Where do we search?' he asked, as they came outside again, and she shook her head.

'I don't know. I can't think. I'm trying to remember. It was ten years ago. I… It's like going back in time. I've lost my bearings.'

'Let's eat, then,' he told her gently, watching her distress with concern. It was early for dinner but they needed to get some fresh air into their lungs after the dreary house, and Tess needed time to get her emotions under control before they tackled the walk, even if she remembered where to go…

Afterwards—after they'd searched—they might not feel like eating at all.

They spread their picnic under a massive gum tree beside the shed. Tess was so depressed she was close to tears. Even Mike's comforting presence, and the way Strop cheered up at the sight of sandwiches, couldn't help this deadening misery.

The sun was sinking lower in the sky and she didn't know where to start, what to do. She was aware that Mike was letting her decide, carefully holding back from what he saw as her domain, and she was grateful that at least she didn't have to concentrate on small talk. It made for a cheerless silence, though.

But it also made for thinking. She was hardly hungry after her meal two hours before. She lay on the picnic rug and watched Mike demolish the picnic—and thought back to when she was sixteen years old and she and her Grandpa had roamed this farm together.

And then…

He was watching her and Mike saw the instant when remembrance hit. The feeling that this place was familiar.

'I remember we walked down by the creek,' she said softly. 'I know… So that's east. If I can start…' She pushed herself up to stand and gaze out to the distant hills.

'Mike, this is probably useless,' she said slowly. 'But… I think I might remember the way. It's a long hike.'

'A hike?' He poured coffee from a Thermos and handed her a mug. 'That's fine by me. This picnic idea was great, but we need a hike now to walk it off, and Strop definitely needs exercise. That's four sandwiches you fed him. Do you remember the way entirely?'

'No.' She shook her head and took a couple of sips of coffee while her eyes still roamed the hills. Her mind was working at a thousand miles an hour, dredging up memories of the past. 'I shouldn't ask you…'

'Ask anything. I want to help—remember?' he told her. 'I don't like not knowing your grandfather's fate almost as much as you don't.' He placed his coffee-mug aside and stood up beside her. 'I've just been hoping if I shut up long enough you might think of something useful to do.'

'I don't know whether I have.'

'But?'

She finished her coffee before she replied. Mike didn't push. 'There's all the time in the world,' he told her.

'That's not true.'

'This is important, Tess,' he said softly. 'There might be

things that need doing, but it's your grandpa's life at stake here. Take all the time you need.'

'I don't understand you,' she said softly. 'Of all the doctors I know, you're not like…' She shook her head, confused, but Mike didn't say more. He knelt and stroked Strop and waited—and finally remembrance came.

'It's coming back,' she whispered. She stared out at the surrounding countryside. It had always been a tussle to keep this land cleared. The little farm had been neglected for the last few years and the bushland was reclaiming its own. There were only Henry's six goats to keep it down.

'It was definitely east of here,' she said surely. 'I'm sure I remember. But the country's rough.'

'I've bought a backpack,' he told her, bending to throw the picnic things back in the basket. 'It's in the car.'

'But… We don't need provisions. It should only take an hour.'

'I'm taking medical equipment,' he said curtly. 'Just in case…'

'But…you still think he's dead?'

'If he was somewhere safe and dry and then collapsed…' He shook his head. 'Who knows? But if there is such a place then I guess there might be a chance. I just wish to hell I'd been able to contact you when this whole mess happened. If I'd known…'

Tess looked curiously up at him. 'You really care,' she said softly—wondering. 'Mike, Grandpa's your patient but he's an old man with nothing whatever to do with you except in a professional capacity. You must have two or three thousand patients on your books, yet you care enough to come out and untether Grandpa's goats and check on his pig at midnight. You care enough to rescue a weird and ridiculous dog from death—and you care enough to come with me now.'

'Yeah, well...' He gave a shrug, feeling embarrassed, and Tess stared some more.

'Thank you,' she said simply.

'No. If I'd contacted you, you might have been able to tell me...'

'I couldn't have described where the cave was, even if I'd thought of it,' she told him. 'I don't know for sure that I can find it now. But I hope...'

She paused and he stood and took her hand strongly in his, pulling her over to stand beside him. His arm came around her waist in a gesture of reassurance and comfort.

'Then let's do that, Tess,' he said gravely. 'Let's hope.'

The cave was further away than she remembered, and by the time they found it the last of the light was fading behind the hills. The sunset had been spectacular, and there was still a fading glow around the sky.

It was instinct rather than knowledge that led her to the cave. She couldn't have described the route if she'd tried. Instead, Mike watched as she simply let her mind drift back to her last summer's afternoon with her grandfather, set her eyes on the hills and let her feet rewalk the route they'd taken. He didn't say a word, sensing her need to let her instincts take over.

And her instincts didn't fail her.

Resting high in the hills in dense bushland, where a small creek trickled down over vast boulders, two massive rocks stood sentinel to a third. The rear rock looked as if it had been almost blasted into the cliff face—a part of a rock wall which was sheer and impregnable. It was only when you slipped behind the front two rocks, then walked around a small outcrop to the side, that a small opening behind the rear rock could be seen. It was just big enough for a man to fit.

Tess found it wordlessly, her face reflecting hope and dread. What if her grandfather wasn't here?

And what if he was?

Strop was sniffing the entrance, his floppy ears pricked as much as it was possible for basset ears ever to prick. Mike looked down at his dog and his face tightened. He placed a hand on Tessa's shoulder and gently propelled her forward. 'It won't get better for the waiting,' he told her softly. 'Come on, Tess. I think your grandfather might be here—and I'm right beside you.'

And thank God he was. There was no way he wanted Tess to face this on her own. He badly wanted to tell her to stay back now—let him find whatever was inside—but he knew she'd have none of that, so he took her hand and Tess let hers lie in his as he led her forward. She had brought Mike here, but now she was clearly grateful to let him be in charge. She squeezed through the gap as his hand pulled her on, and he could feel the tension in her fingers.

Inside, the cave was so big it might almost have been the vaulting roof of a cathedral. There was a crevice above that, open to the evening sky, and the rosy hue of sunset shimmered around the smooth rock walls and lit the cavern in a dim and misty haze.

Tess didn't waste time admiring the beauty. At the rear of the cave there was a chamber, dry and filled with sand, closed to the weather but just open enough to the light so as not to be frightening. It was a comfortable place for a wounded thing to lie and tend its wounds.

Courage was no longer an issue. She dropped Mike's hand and stumbled quickly across the rough cave floor to reach the inner entrance, with Strop and Mike left to follow.

And inside she found her grandfather.

CHAPTER THREE

FOR a moment Tess and Mike thought Henry was dead.

For one long moment, she stood in the small doorway while her eyes adjusted to the dark. Her grandfather was huddled in a far corner, and he wasn't moving.

She gave a gasp of dismay, but then Mike pushed her aside, striding across the sand to stoop over the huddled figure. He lifted a limp wrist and turned to stare at Tess in the gloom.

'He's alive, Tess. Help me.'

'Alive…' Somehow Tess made her legs carry her over to where Mike was kneeling in the sand. 'Oh, Mike, alive…'

Strop fell back. He'd been trained to do this. He wasn't all stupid. When Mike's voice hit a certain tense pitch, Strop knew enough to shove his butt down and wait.

'How…? How…?' Tess stared down.

'He's unconscious, Tess, but there's a heartbeat. He's so dry. Hell, feel his skin! His mouth is parched and his tongue is swollen. You'll find a torch in my pack, and a saline pack.' His hands were running over the old man as he spoke, moving with care and concern. 'For him to have been here… He must have been here all this time!'

Tess was hauling Mike's backpack from his shoulders and fumbling inside for a torch. The flashlight rested right on the top. She flicked it on and directed it down at her grandfather's face.

The sight before her must be a dreadful shock, Mike thought grimly. Tess hadn't seen her grandfather for ten years and Henry then would have been a vigorous seventy-three-year-old—healthy and strong and full of life.

Now… The eighty-three-year-old man lying on the sand seemed drained of everything. His skin was as white as alabaster under his tan, and it stretched across his old bones as if it were parchment. Henry's eyes had sunk into their sockets and were staring sightlessly at the opposite wall. His cheeks were gaunt hollows and his lips were so dry they'd cracked, bled, half healed and cracked over and over again.

'Find me a swab, Dr Westcott.' Mike cast a glance up at Tess, hoping like hell she wouldn't faint on him. His voice sliced across Tessa's distress like a knife. 'Tessa, you're wasting time. I need a swab and then I need help to set up a saline drip. Fast. We haven't found him to let him die now.'

'Oh, Mike… He looks so dreadful.' He looked like death!

But Tess didn't intend fainting. She took a deep, steadying breath and somewhere in that breath she turned from a frightened grandchild into a competent doctor. The fact that this was her beloved grandpa was thrust aside. Henry was an emergency patient, dying under their hands.

'What do you think—?'

'He's dehydrated,' Mike snapped. 'You just have to see his lips… If he's lain here for days with no water… Everything else can wait, Tess, but we have to get fluids in.'

'OK.' She was already moving, sorting out swabs and syringes and tubing from Mike's bag and handing them across in the dim torchlight.

Mike knew there were two people inside her head now. One was Tessa Westcott, scared-stiff granddaughter, and the other was Dr Westcott, efficient medical practicioner. For now, though, she was efficient and she was professional. The first lady had been sent outside for the duration to wring her hands in private. Henry needed Dr Westcott now, and so did Mike.

Two minutes later they had saline flowing. Mike had everything they needed in his backpack, and Tess found it, prepared it and handed it across at need as if she were in a properly equipped Casualty cubicle, rather than squatting in an ill-lit cave. Mike adjusted the saline to full flow. He took the stethoscope that Tess offered and held it to Henry's chest—and then finally he sank back on his heels and looked across at her.

'We have a massive chest infection here, and it's no wonder after this long without attention,' he told her. 'There's a mobile phone in my bag, Tess. Hand it to me and we'll call in help. The ambulance boys will bring a stretcher in and carry him out.'

'If it's not too late…'

With everything they could do having now been done, it was time now for Dr Westcott to revert again to being just plain Tessa—and just plain scared. The theatre door had been opened and the relatives ushered in. Tess was now Tessa, the relative. She looked down at the man lying on the sand, and her face twisted. 'Oh, Grandpa, don't you dare die. Not when we're so close…'

'Don't give up, Tess,' Mike said roughly, putting a hand out and taking hers in a strong, hard grip. 'He's alive and that's more than we hoped for. We've had a miracle. Let's see if we can score another one.' He gave her a tight, strained smile, and then turned to his phone.

He watched her sit and listen while he barked orders to unknown people at the end of the telephone link, and her hand stroked her grandfather's face as she waited. That he'd been here for so long—alone. Her hand went down and gripped the fingers of her grandfather's hand, willing life into his veins. By her side, Strop nosed forward and gave her spare hand a lick, and Tessa's strained look eased, as though that one lick had been immeasurably—stupidly—comforting.

'Grandpa... I'm here, Grandpa,' she faltered. 'It's Tessa. I've come home.'

Mike's eyes never left her face as he spoke into the phone. Home...It sounded right.

That was a crazy thought! This wasn't Tessa's home. She had no life here, and why such a thought had the power to jolt him he didn't know. Tessa had nothing to do with this valley—nothing to do with him.

He opened his mouth to speak, but as he did he saw Tessa's eyes widen as she stared down at Henry. He glanced down, and a muscle moved almost imperceptibly at the corner of Henry's right eye.

'Grandpa...' She leaned closer, and Mike stared, unable to believe he'd seen the movement. He let the phone drop to his side. He wasn't imagining it—Tess had seen the movement, too. He took Henry's other hand.

'Henry, it's Mike Llewellyn here.' He flashed an uncertain look at Tessa, unsure how she was reacting, and then he fixed all his concentration on Henry. 'It's Doc Llewellyn. You're quite safe, Henry, and your granddaughter's here, too. Tessa's come all the way from the States to find you. We've been searching for days, but no one but Tessa knew where the cave was. Now we'll stay with you until we can stretcher you out to hospital. You're quite safe.'

Henry's right eye fluttered open and he saw them.

His gaze wandered from Tess to Mike...and then back to Tess. It was clear that focussing was an enormous effort. There was confusion in his look. His left eye stayed closed, but the hand Tess was holding tightened convulsively.

Henry's lips moved, ever so faintly, and Tess bent to hear.

'Tess...'

The word was blurred to the point of being unintelligible, spoken through one side of his mouth and with a chest that rattled and wheezed and barely functioned, but they knew it for what it was. Tessa's eyes filled with tears.

'It's really me, Grandpa,' she murmured. 'We're here. Mike and I are here.'

'Mike and I…' It sounded good. It sounded reassuring, even to Mike's ears.

'Don't worry, Grandpa,' she said. 'We'll have you in hospital in no time.'

'S-stay.'

'I will.' It was a vow, and suddenly, as she made it, Mike knew the vow she was making wasn't a light one. She'd stay.

'I'll see that she stays, Mr Westcott,' he said softly. 'Don't you worry about that.'

Now why on earth had he said that?

'She's gorgeous.'

'Yes.' There was no doubt in his mind just who they were talking about.

It was six in the morning. Mike had snatched a few short hours' sleep, interrupted at two a.m. by a child with croup and at five by a drip which had packed up, and at six he hit the hospital kitchen for strong black coffee. Bill had arrived a few minutes earlier and the charge nurse was wrapping himself around a plate of porridge.

'Will she stay?' Bill asked.

'What do you mean, will she stay? I guess she'll stay until Henry decides whether to live.'

'But will he live?' The news of Henry's discovery had hit Bill the minute he'd entered the hospital. Pre-dawn or not, Bill guessed it'd be all over the valley by now.

'Maybe.'

'But maybe not?'

'I can't tell how bad the stroke was,' Mike said. 'Not until we get him rehydrated, get the intravenous antibiotics working on his chest and get him over his shock. He's had a hell of an ordeal and he has a massive chest infection.'

'He looks dreadful.'

'You've seen him?'

'I poked my head around the door when I got in.'

'Are his obs OK? They were settling when I left him at midnight and no one's rung to say there's a problem. There's been no change?'

'Tessa's happy with them.'

'Tessa...' Mike stared. 'Tessa's asleep. I set Hannah to special him.'

'Tessa's sitting by his bedside,' Bill said blandly. 'Hannah's down in the nursery with Billy and his croup. Billy's a real handful—he's been giving the night staff hell—and Tessa told her she wasn't needed. She'd look after her grandpa herself.'

'But I told Tessa to go to bed.'

'She's not the sort of girl to follow orders,' Bill said, a faint grin playing over his face. 'At least, not unless she agrees with them.'

'She's exhausted,' Mike said grimly. 'That's stupid.'

'Is she as tired as you, then?'

'I'm not tired.'

'Oh, no?' Bill leaned back and folded his arms across his large chest. 'You've had on average of—let me guess—about four hours' sleep a night for the last two weeks. And you're telling me you're not tired.'

'I can cope.'

'But Tessa Westcott's another doctor,' Bill said thoughtfully, his calm, intelligent eyes thoughtful. 'You know, if there's one thing we need around here, it's another doctor.'

'We don't need Tessa.'

'Mike, we'd accept Doris the pig if only she had a medical degree,' Bill told him bluntly. 'And your Tessa has a medical degree. Mike, boy, you have a duty here.'

'What do you mean?'

'I mean you have enough address to charm a whole harem of Tessas.' Bill held up a hand to silence Mike's involuntary protest. 'Now, don't deny it. I've seen you woo old ladies till their pulse rates shoot through the roof. They come in droves to get their flu injections, and I'll tell you what—it's not fear of flu that does it. And the old ladies have nothing on the young ones. You create havoc with my nursing staff—and all they get for their pains is a hopeless case of unrequited love. Or lust.' He grinned. 'Or maybe both.'

'Bill...'

'Hey, we could make this a proper partnership here,' Bill continued, thinking this through. 'Now, look, Mike. Be serious here. You know, if you snap your fingers, you could date any single lady in this valley. Even my Barbara says you make her pulse rate wobble—and she's the mother of my four kids. Yet you never go out with anyone more than twice. So...' He held up his hand again to silence Mike's interruption.

'No. Shut up and let me speak. So therefore...it stands to reason that you've been saving yourself. And I reckon the lady you've been saving yourself for has just entered your orbit.'

'You have to be kidding!'

'Would I joke about anything as serious as matchmaking?' Bill demanded. He grinned and lifted one finger on his raised hand. 'You listen to Uncle Bill, my boy. One. The lady is seriously desirable. Even I can see that, despite my commitment to my Barbara. If Barbara can look sideways at Mike Llewellyn, I can look sideways at Henry Westcott's granddaughter.'

Then another finger went up. Bill was on a roll here and

he wasn't to be stopped. 'Two... The lady is a qualified medical practitioner.' A third finger. 'Three. The lady has a need to stay in the valley. All you have to do is keep Henry alive and needful of family. And four...' He said this as Mike rose and stalked to the door. 'Four, you need to be married, Mike Llewellyn. You need a wife and a few kids and a mortgage just like the rest of us.'

And as Mike walked out and slammed the door behind him, Bill's face split into a huge grin.

Because Mike Llewellyn didn't look angry. He just looked confused.

Bloody hell! Could they really have something going here?

'I just might have another plate of porridge, Mrs Thompson,' Bill said to the hospital cook. 'I'd drink champagne if I could, but porridge will have to do. Believe it or not, we might have Dr Mike seriously interested in something other than work!'

Dr Mike wasn't seriously interested. Or...was he? He did his ward rounds with a strange feeling hanging over his head.

Normally his mind was totally on his job. Apart from his devotion to one crazy dog—and the small matter of his love affair with his car—he gave one hundred per cent concentration to his patients.

Now, though... His patients sensed that there was something different about Mike this morning. He was just as attentive, but there was an air of bewilderment about him.

'Are you worried about Henry Westcott?' Sandra Lessing asked. She'd been the cause of his lack of sleep the night before last. Now she was sitting up in bed feeding her day-old son, and, like every patient in the hospital, she was agog with the news of Henry being found.

'I guess.' Mike shrugged and smiled down at the downy

little head nestled against his mother's breast. 'I don't know, Sandra. There's no way of telling just how bad the damage is yet.'

'He was so lucky to be found.' Sandra's family farmed a property on the other side of the ridge to Henry's and she knew at first hand just how hard the country around here was to search. 'If it wasn't for his granddaughter coming back...' She looked at Mike, her eyes twinkling. 'She's really something, isn't she? Bill introduced me to Tessa yesterday when he was showing her over the hospital. She's just lovely.'

'Yes,' Mike said shortly, but he didn't want to think of how lovely Tessa was. He needed to concentrate on work. 'Sandra, can we pop your son back into his crib so I can give his mum the once-over?'

'Sure. He's not feeding any more. He just likes cuddling.' She planted a kiss on her son's head. 'Give me two minutes and I'll cuddle you again,' she promised. She lay back and eyed Mike again, her eyes speculative. 'I know what,' she said. 'How about when I get home I organise a dinner? It can be a thank-you dinner for you for delivering Toby and a welcome dinner for Tessa all in one. How would that be?'

'If all goes well, Henry will be on the mend and Tess will be back in the States by the time you get home,' Mike said shortly.

'Not if this valley has anything to do with it.' Sandra grinned hugely. 'The whole valley's talking about Tessa Westcott, and the whole valley thinks she might be a really good thing.'

'Sandra...'

'We'll work on it,' she said placidly. 'Give us time. Like about a day or so!'

* * *

By the time Mike reached the little room he used as Intensive Care, he was starting to feel as if he didn't want to enter. The whole hospital, staff and patients alike, had started to have really strange ideas about Tessa Westcott, and he wasn't enjoying them. His normal cheerful smile had faded and he approached ICU with misgivings.

Hell, what was happening here? Sure, Tessa was one different woman and, sure, the valley needed another doctor, but Tessa lived in the States, for heaven's sake! She had nothing to do with him. She was here for maybe a week.

Which was all very sensible, he thought, but logic didn't account for the way his heart lurched when he opened Henry's door.

Tess was dozing with her head on Henry's counterpane. Her wonderful hair was spread out in a flaming halo on the white bedlinen. She was wearing exactly the same clothes she'd had on when they'd brought Henry in.

It had been a really major job to get Henry out of there. The ambulance boys had had to traipse over rough country to reach them, and then there were only two of them. They hadn't waited for back-up because Mike had wanted oxygen and equipment fast. Henry's lungs were barely functioning.

Then to get a stretcher over rough ground with only two stretcher-bearers had been risky, but Tess hadn't waited for back-up even then. No way. In the end, Mike and Tess had taken a stretcher corner each to give them four bearers and make the stretcher stable.

'I can do it,' she'd told them when they'd said they'd wait for help. 'He's my grandpa, I'm as strong as a horse and I don't have to use my bad arm. Just shut up and let's get him somewhere safe.'

So she'd done it, but heaven knew how. Even if she'd been fit, it would have been harder for Tess than for the men because she was inches shorter and, try as they might, they hadn't been able to compensate entirely—but even though she'd carried with her good arm she was still so badly bruised it must have hurt.

It must have hurt like crazy, but she wouldn't listen to their protests, and it was the two ambulance men who'd decreed they stop and rest every two hundred yards or so—not Tessa.

She had an iron will. If things needed doing, Tess Westcott just went ahead and did them.

She was such a kid, he thought. From where he was standing, with her head resting on her grandfather's bed and in her grimy jeans and T-shirt, she looked all of fourteen years old.

Hell. Hell!

Get a hold on yourself, Mike Llewellyn, he told himself harshly. She's only a woman, and you know your vow. So keep your thoughts to yourself. Hands off.

Easier said than done.

He had work to do here, he reminded himself. So do it!

He stepped forward and put a hand on her shoulder. Tessa's eyes flew wide in panic, and she'd half risen from the bed before she realised he was smiling and shaking his head.

'It's OK, Tess. There's no need to hit the panic button.' He lifted the observation chart from the end of the bed and studied it while she regained her composure. 'This looks great,' he told her. 'I wouldn't have disturbed you but I wanted to talk to you before I started work for the day.'

She blinked, rubbed her eyes and checked the clock. It was seven a.m.

'So…where's your dog?'

'He's fast asleep. Where you should be.'

'You're here to do your ward rounds?' she said cautiously, and he grinned. He lifted Henry's wrist and nodded in satisfaction when Henry didn't stir. Like Strop, Henry was soundly asleep. It looked like it'd take a bomb to wake him. He had fluids aboard, he had a comfortable bed and he had his granddaughter beside him. There was nothing he needed now but sleep.

'I've done my ward rounds.' He smiled down at her and the feeling of weird intimacy grew stronger. It was almost as if he'd known her in another life. In fact, it was just plain crazy! 'The patients in this hospital are used to early morning calls,' he said, trying to keep his voice steady. 'I left you until last.'

'Until last!' She grimaced. 'Gee, thanks, Dr Llewellyn. If this is a late call, remind me never to get sick in this hospital. I like my sleep.'

'I thought you'd be grateful.' His lazy smile deepened. 'You can now do what most of my patients do,' he told her kindly. 'Enjoy the dawn chorus, have breakfast and then go back to getting some beauty sleep. That means go back to bed. You shouldn't be here, Tess. You know we'll take care of Henry. He's sound asleep. The saline's working, he's rehydrating nicely and the antibiotic should kick in within twelve hours. With the fluid on board, he's getting better by the minute.'

'There's no fluid output yet.'

'You wouldn't expect that,' he said, and he had his voice under control again. 'I'm hoping we got to him before there's any long-term kidney damage.'

'Even if there's no kidney damage, it's obvious he's had a stroke,' Tess said grimly. 'And we don't know how badly he'll be affected.'

'No. We don't know that, and he's far too weak to do any testing yet. But there are some good signs, Tess. The fact that he's still alive now is a very good sign.'

'Yeah, terrific.'

'I mean it,' he said seriously. 'You realise Henry must

have had the stroke five days ago. It's obvious he has a hemiplegia. At the moment, the left side of his body seems almost totally paralysed. He's slurring his speech and he appears confused.

'But he's survived for five days, Tess, and the only way he can have done that is if he's had water. Also, there's a pressure wound on his hip but it's not a major one. It doesn't look like he's lain in the one position for five days. Therefore he must have been able to drag himself out of the cave and down to the creek and back again. If he'd been totally paralysed for five days, he'd be dead by now.'

'So what are you saying?'

'I'm saying that once he's got his fluid balance back to normal—once he's recovered from shock and exhaustion and we get on top of his chest infection—he may well make a full recovery from his stroke,' he told her. 'The fact that he was able to say your name last night was amazing, and even though he hasn't spoken since the muscles must be still operating. That's all I wanted to tell you, Dr Westcott. I'm sure you'll figure it out for yourself, but it might take time and I don't want a gloomy face scaring Henry into another stroke.'

'My face is not gloomy,' she said before she could stop herself, and he grinned.

'Well, maybe you're right,' he agreed. 'In fact, it's not gloomy at all.' He smiled down at her, and Tess found herself flushing under his careful scrutiny. 'But fearful, though,' he amended gently. 'Fearful of your grandfather's future.'

Her momentary lightness faded. 'He's at risk of another stroke, Mike. Isn't he?'

She didn't need to ask. She knew the odds.

'He is,' he said bluntly. There was no use giving false reassurance. 'But you know we've started him on heparin as well as digoxin. I'm sure much of his weakness now is due to being left so long without attention rather than the stroke itself. I'd say, with good rehabilitation, we've a very strong chance of getting Henry back to his beloved farm. Between us, I think we've done an excellent night's work.'

'I guess…'

He looked down at Tess and his smile died. He could see what she was thinking.

Henry had been so near death. To have pulled him back…well, there were no guarantees now that Henry would be grateful—especially if he was left with a body that wouldn't do as he commanded. To be left with partial paralysis…

'I'm telling you, Tess, there can't be major paralysis,' he said gently, and his hand came down on the bed to cover hers. It was an unconscious action which he did with many patients, but he was suddenly acutely aware of the contact. He was acutely aware of the linking of their two hands. But he didn't pull away.

'No, but…'

'But?'

'He won't be out of trouble in a week,' she said sadly. 'Or even a month. He can't be. So what happens now?' She stared down at her grandfather's gaunt face and a muscle worked at the side of her mouth.

'I won't be able to return to the States now,' she said at last. 'I'll have to stay.'

Mike frowned, but he was aware of a tiny jerk inside him. It was like something deep within was really pleased with the words he'd just heard.

Go for practicalities…

'Where does that leave you?' he asked. 'Are you on leave from your job?'

'I quit to come here.'

'You quit?'

She looked up at him then, and her mouth twisted into

a wry smile. She hadn't moved her hand. It was still under his, and for the life of her she couldn't find the energy to move it.

This man was her only comfort in all this.

'It sounds dramatic, doesn't it?' She shrugged and managed a grin. 'It's not. I've been working in emergency medicine for the last two years. It's been exciting but now... I've had enough excitement. I'm moving into family medicine.'

'You have a job to go to?'

'I've applied for a heap of positions in the States,' she told him. 'I was really just waiting to hear if—or where—I've been accepted when I had to leave to come here.' Her gorgeous grin flashed out again. 'If you must know, I'm expecting a pile of job offers—with salary commensurate with my expected lifestyle, of course—to be waiting when I get home. So it seemed only fair to tell the hospital I wouldn't be back.'

'So you're a free agent?'

'I guess. Until I have to start working to pay for food.' She smiled again, that blindingly attractive smile that almost shook his socks off. 'It seems to me that if Grandpa's farming one sow, eight piglets and six goats and not a lot else, then I might be in trouble if I expect the farm to pay for my keep—and I don't much fancy living on piglet.'

'No.' Mike gave Tess a smile in return, but his mind was racing.

Bill's words were echoing strongly in his mind. 'You have a duty here...' And 'We'd accept Doris the pig if only she had a medical degree.'

Hell!

The room was suddenly way too small.

The door opened. It was Bill, with a junior nurse in tow. Just as well. His blood pressure was climbing through the roof as he tried to think this through.

'We've come to do the real work around here,' Bill said cheerfully. The charge nurse looked from Tess to Mike with amused speculation and then watched as they self-consciously disengaged hands. Hmm. Things were moving along nicely here. 'Doctors aren't wanted,' he added, kindly forbearing to comment on the hand-holding. 'Unless you have anything urgent to do here…'

'I'm just going,' Mike said curtly, in a voice that made Bill frown. 'Let me know when he wakes, Bill.'

'I'm staying,' Tess said.

'No.' Mike shook his head. 'No way. You need to sleep.'

'I can sleep here,' she told him. 'I want to be here when Grandpa wakes.'

'Tess…'

'Butt out, Dr Llewellyn,' she said firmly. 'This is my grandpa. Go find a grandpa of your own.'

'He has ten or so grandpas—grandmas, too—booked into surgery this morning,' Bill said, grinning again. 'He can choose.'

'There you are, then,' she said kindly. 'Bye-bye, Dr Llewellyn. Off you go and care for the medical needs of the valley grandpas and grandmas *en masse*. We'll cope with this one ourselves.'

And he was left with nothing to do but leave.

It'd be evening before he had an excuse to make another trip to Henry's room, he thought as he closed the door reluctantly behind him. Unless Henry woke…

He hoped to hell that Henry woke. And it wasn't just for Henry's sake, either.

Mike worked flat out for the whole day, but Tess hardly left her grandfather's side. Bill persuaded her to shower and change while he took over her watch, but apart from that she hardly left his side.

'It's just so hard,' she told Bill, her voice strained. 'I'm just trying to figure what to do for the best here. Maybe Mike's right and he'll make a full recovery, but meanwhile he can't go back to the farm to live alone. Where's the nearest rehabilitation unit?'

'Melbourne.'

'So unless he has someone at home to care for him—someone to help him do his exercises and make sure he's safe—then he'll have to go to the city. A few months of institutionalised living will make him unlikely to be able to care for himself again, and meanwhile someone has to care for the farm.'

'The farm could be sold.'

'No. That's unthinkable.'

'Why?'

Tess thought that one through. 'I don't know,' she said slowly. 'Or maybe… Maybe I do. From the time I was little, my dad talked of this place as home. He was homesick, but too pig-headed and proud to ever think about returning. Instead, he passed on his love to me. By the time I saw the farm and met Grandpa I was sixteen and felt like the place was where I belonged, and the three months I spent here as a teenager cemented that impression. I love it.'

'You're a farm girl?' There were things that needed doing, but still Bill lingered. Tessa was desperate to talk to someone and he let her talk.

'No way. I was raised in the city, but maybe I'm a farm girl at heart. That was why I decided to go into family medicine—so I could move to the country.'

He quirked an eyebrow. *'Eat a lot of peaches?'*

Tess grinned. 'OK, so I'm an idealistic twit!'

He smiled. 'Don't knock it. Idealistic twits are valued in this hospital.'

'You mean, that's what Mike is?'

'Hey, I didn't say that.'

'No, but...' Tess hesitated. 'Maybe you don't have to. Mike has a medical practice which must take all his time and more, but somehow he organised his work so he could spend a night searching for Grandpa. When we arrived back here last night, there were two more patients to be seen before he went to bed, and I don't have to ask why he was up so early this morning. He was paying now for his time off last night. He's some doctor. He has the most wonderful car and the craziest dog...'

'Sounds like he's won a heart,' Bill said with a chuckle. Then, as a buzzer sounded down the hall, he grimaced and waved a hand in farewell. 'Duty calls. I'll leave you to your plans, then, Dr Westcott, and I'll be very interested to know what they are.'

'And so will I,' Tess muttered as the door closed behind him. 'Because if you're making plans around Mike, then you're an airdreamer, Tess Westcott.'

And then she swerved to look down at the bed. Henry was stirring—and he was watching her.

'An airdreamer...' Henry's voice was a slurred whisper, but it was enough. Tessa's face burst into joy, and she buried her face into his shoulder.

'Oh, Grandpa...'

'I thought you were a dream,' he whispered into her mass of hair. 'My Tess. An airdream... Is that the same thing?'

'Nope.' She lifted her head and looked at him, long and lovingly. 'I'm real. I'm a hundred per cent accounted for. I was just making plans.'

'Plans?'

'Plans for me. Plans for you. And...' she took a deep breath '...plans for Mike Llewellyn.'

'I see.' The ghost of a twisted smile played on Henry's face.

'I bet you don't see at all.' She lifted her grandfather's

gnarled old hand and rubbed it against her cheek. 'I don't see things very clearly myself. I only see that you're alive. I have you back again.'

'And you're here, girl. If you knew how much I'd wanted you...'

'Oh, Grandpa.' Her voice broke with emotion. Then she caught herself and managed a glare. 'Hey, haven't I always told you to be careful? What do you mean by taking yourself off to that cave to have a stroke?'

'Is that what I've had?' The left side of Henry's mouth wasn't working properly. Each word was a twisted effort. 'A stroke?'

'Looks like it.' Tessa's voice softened and her hand gripped her grandfather's with love. 'It's a mild one, but definitely a stroke.'

'Yeah?'

'Yeah. So, why the cave, Grandpa?'

'I was feeling lousy,' he told her, his mouth forming each word with care. 'I had a king-sized headache I couldn't shake. I knew you were ringing Saturday night so I took the afternoon to visit the cave. Just in case...' He grimaced. 'It was like...if it was something serious I could say good-bye.'

'So if it was something serious you could lie for five days without medical help!'

'Do you have to be bossy?' Henry's voice was a frail thread, and she chuckled.

'Yeah. You know me, Grandpa.'

'The original Miss Bossy-Boots.'

He fell silent, exhausted, and it was ten minutes before he spoke again. Mike had told her to ring him when Henry woke but Tess resisted. There was time enough in the future to let the world break in. For now she was content to be alone with Henry.

'So what plans are you making for Mike Llewellyn?' he whispered at last, and she started.

'Oh, nothing.'

'Tell me.'

'Well, it's just that Mike is overworked, over-generous and over-endowed with niceness—plus, he has more than his fair share of good looks.' She twinkled. 'And I need to stay here and look after you but I also need an income. So…'

'So?'

'So I might just have chosen myself a partner,' she said simply. 'If he'll have me.'

'And if he won't?'

'Then we'll just have to think of a way to make him change his mind.'

CHAPTER FOUR

BY TWO that afternoon Mike was starting to get anxious that Henry hadn't woken. When he finished surgery he intended to go back to the hospital, but just as he was leaving the clinic there was an urgent call from Eileen Fraser. Reg Fraser was close to death.

Reg had terminal lung cancer. He'd been dying for months, cared for by three sisters of whom Eileen, at ninety, was the oldest. The Misses Fraser had taken care of Reg around the clock every since he'd become ill, and he couldn't have had better care anywhere.

Now it sounded as if the end was very, very close. Eileen was distraught. No, they didn't want Reg to be admitted to hospital, not now, but, yes, they needed help. For the first time since he'd become ill, Reg seemed distressed.

Mike had no choice. He packed his bag and headed for the Fraser farm, and this time he left Strop behind.

Reg wasn't distressed. He'd lapsed into a coma and started Cheyne-Stokes breathing. Mike reassured the elderly ladies that all this meant was that Reg was so deeply unconscious his breathing was almost a muscle spasm rather than the effect of a conscious message to the brain. He died half an hour after Mike arrived—a peaceful, settled death that was just how Mike had hoped it would be.

'Oh, Reg…' Miss Eileen fluttered forward as her brother's breathing finally ceased. The sisters kissed their brother in turn and then fetched the coverlet that, Mike gathered, they'd spent the last six months embroidering for just this occasion.

He couldn't leave. He spent the next two hours drinking

tea and eating home-made biscuits while the sisters went through every aspect of Reg's illness with him, step by step. It was an important time for them if they were to come to terms with what had happened, and Mike couldn't begrudge it to them. The undertaker was booked to call later that evening. There was no hurry. No hurry at all...

Mike ended up looking through faded family photographs with the sisters commentating. 'This is Reg on his first pony,' and 'This is Reg on his first day at school' and 'See how much taller Reg was than our father...'

By the time he could charitably leave it was five o'clock and evening surgery patients were already queuing. Still he couldn't return to visit Henry. He made a fast phone call to Bill back at the hospital.

'Henry's awake and doing fine,' Bill told him. 'Tessa's finally agreed to have some sleep. I'm going off duty now. If you like, I'll feed Strop for you before I go so there's no urgent reason why you should race back to the hospital.'

No. Mike had to agree—especially since Tessa was now asleep.

That was stupid, he told himself, but even so it made the hours spent seeing his evening surgery patients pass faster than if he'd thought Tess was sitting by Henry's side, waiting.

Was it his imagination, or were there more patients than normal? At eight o'clock Mike finally finished. He came out to find his receptionist replacing the telephone. She sighed as she saw him.

'For heaven's sake, Mike, there're rumours flying all over the valley that there's a new doctor starting work. I've had more than ten patients ring to ask if they can have an appointment with the new doctor. When I say she's not working here they're disappointed, but then they can't admit they don't really need to see a doctor so they make a time to see you.' She gave an apologetic smile. 'I'm sorry,

Mike, but you'll have sore throats and pap smears all tomorrow morning.'

'Great.' Mike groaned. 'Just what I need.' And then he frowned. 'Why the hell does everyone think we're getting a new doctor?'

'Well, because of Tess, of course.'

'Tess...?'

'Don't act daft.' Maureen, his receptionist, was fifty years old and up to every trick in the book. There was no way patients could pull the wool over her eyes, and neither could Mike. 'If you're not thinking of Tessa Westcott then there's something wrong with you. Every male nurse in the place...every orderly...the ambulance boys...they're all talking about her, and if any valley male hasn't seen her yet then they're busy trying to. Are you thinking of offering her a job?'

'No.'

'Why not?'

'Maureen, Tess works in the States. She's a US citizen. For heaven's sake, she won't even have Australian registration.'

'Well, I could fix that in a flash,' Maureen told him. 'Just say the word. You know we qualify as a remote district. If anyone's stupid enough to want to work here, and their medical diploma isn't paid for in Timbuctoo petrodollars, the medical board says thank you very much and welcome. And if Tess hasn't Australian citizenship I could fix that, too. Her dad's Australian.'

'This is ridiculous,' Mike said flatly. 'She doesn't want to come here to work. She's here to visit her grandfather. That's all. We're fine on our own.'

'No, we're not fine,' Maureen said frankly. 'Not now. When you first started here you could handle the work, but that was because most patients took themselves to the city for treatment. Now they know they can get hospital care and superb medical treatment right here so they're staying. More and more, they're staying. Which leaves you, Mike Llewellyn, working your socks off.'

'Hard work doesn't hurt me.'

'Not for the short term, maybe. But for the long term… You need some social life.'

'I have a social life.'

'Oh, yeah…' Maureen jeered gently and her motherly face creased into lecture mode. 'You know you haven't had time to have one serious girlfriend since you returned to the valley, and at your age…'

'Maureen, I don't need a girlfriend.'

'Of course you do.' She smiled. 'And, of course, you need another doctor. And here is this Tessa. I haven't met her yet, but if Bill's report is anything to go on… Well, you may be able to kill two birds with one stone. Girlfriend and workmate all in one.'

'Maureen…'

'Yes?' She dimpled up at him.

'Butt out.'

'Yes, sir.' She put her hand up in a mock salute. 'So I can't ring the medical board, then?'

'No.'

'Rats. And it's the weekend now, too. Still…' Her smile deepened. 'I guess it can wait until Monday.'

'It won't be happening on Monday.'

'We'll see.' Her twinkle refused to be suppressed. 'Bill says this Tessa's a very determined young lady. Like a bulldozer, he says. Oh, and by the way…' With difficulty she forced herself back to business.

'Yes?'

'Speaking of love life, there was a call for you from Liz Hayes. She's been trying to ring you all week.'

'Liz.' He frowned, trying to concentrate on something

other than Tessa. Liz was the local shire engineer. 'What does Liz want?'

'She wants you to take her to the shire ball tomorrow night.'

'The ball…'

'You need to go,' Barbara said patiently. 'Everyone does. I put it in your diary a month ago.'

'Yeah. Right.'

'Liz knows you'll be there in name only,' Barbara told her. 'She says she'll meet you there and your name will be beside hers on the supper table. It's the same table as the shire president. Oh, and she says if you can squeeze in time for a couple of dances, she'd be grateful.'

Maureen sighed as she watched him think this through. The valley girls knew what to expect from Mike now. It gave them a certain amount of social cachet to be his date for the evening, but if a girl expected him to pick her up, she'd be two hours late every time—if he came at all. There was always a medical imperative. And even if he came, there was a risk of one lumbering basset-hound in the passenger seat.

But still they tried. He was a great dancing partner and if they were lucky enough for the phone to stay silent and for him to be dogless, there was the ride home in his gorgeous Aston Martin, and maybe a kiss…

But nothing more.

'Yeah, you're right,' he said abstractedly. 'The council supports the hospital so I need to go to the ball. Tell Liz it's fine. I'll meet her there.'

'You wouldn't like to ring her and tell her yourself?' Maureen asked, but she asked as if it was a forlorn hope.

'Why?' He frowned, lifting his list of house calls and leafing through the pile.

'Because one of these days you won't want your secretary organising your love life,' she retorted.

'Why would I change now?' He grinned and pocketed his list. 'You do a fantastic job. My love life is entirely satisfactory, thanks to you, Maureen.' He leaned over and gave her a kiss on the top of the head, then took himself out to his Aston Martin, which—apart from Strop—was the love of his life and the *only* love of his life. He had house calls to do.

It was ten that night before he returned to the hospital and he was starting to feel the strain. In fact, he was dead beat.

Strop was already asleep and not the least bit interested in asking how his day had gone.

'Half your luck,' he told the dog, but Strop didn't stir.

He did a cursory ward round in the darkened hospital, checking obs and organising changes of treatment with night staff. He left Henry till last, as he wasn't worried. He'd been assured at each of his phone checks that Henry was going well.

He opened the ward door softly, and found Louise, one of the night nurses, sitting beside the bed. Until Henry's pulse settled to a strong beat—until the chest infection was under control and the fluids were completely restored—Mike had requested he be specialled.

But… He'd sort of hoped Tessa might be here.

She wasn't, and he had to swallow a lurch of disappointment.

Louise looked up in query as he entered. She smiled and handed him the obs chart.

'Things are looking good here, Doctor,' she said primly. Louise was that sort of nurse. Primness was her forte. 'Mr Westcott's awake.'

'Are you, then, Henry?' Mike smiled and walked over to the bed. Henry's old face was gaunt and shrunken on the whiteness of the pillows but, in the dim night light,

Mike could see his old eyes looking up with sharp intelligence.

'Mike…'

Mike gripped his hand and held on.

'Welcome back to the land of the living, sir,' he said softly.

'It was thanks to you…'

Henry's voice was amazingly strong, considering. Mike gave an inward sigh of relief. Hell, after all he'd gone through, the man must be as tough as old boots.

'Your rescue was thanks to your granddaughter,' he told him. 'Tessa's one determined lady.'

'She is that. My Tess…' The old man closed his eyes for a long moment, and Mike thought he was drifting back to sleep, but the hand gripping his was still strong.

Tomorrow they'd run a few tests. They'd see then what the damage was. He wasn't moving his left arm, Mike noticed. Still, if the speech was only slightly affected…

'Tess says she intends staying,' Henry said, and Mike shook himself. God, he was tired. If he didn't watch himself he'd be asleep before Henry.

'Does she?'

'She can't stay long term,' Henry whispered fretfully.

'I guess she'll stay until you're back on your feet.'

'Yeah, but…I've only got one foot.' Henry managed a twisted smile. 'Can't feel the other.'

'That'll come back. I promise you, Henry. You'll need physiotherapy but we'll get movement back.' If Henry was speaking already, it was a safe enough promise.

'But not tomorrow.'

'No, sir,' Mike agreed gravely. 'Not tomorrow.'

'Tess says she's quit her job in the States.'

'She told me that.'

'Will you take her on here?'

Silence.

'Mike?' Henry prodded.

'This is all a bit sudden,' Mike said at last. 'I think we need to talk about it, but not yet. There's time, sir, to be making decisions about the future when you're on the road to recovery.'

'But I want to know now,' Henry fretted, and under Mike's hand his pulse rate went up. 'I've been lying here thinking. I should have died in that damned cave. There's nothing left for me, and my body's failing. But if Tess came back…'

'Tess has her own life in the States.'

'She says she wants to stay,' Henry told him, and Louise cast an urgent look at Mike. The old man was getting agitated, and agitation was the last thing he needed.

He knew that, but to make such a promise just to calm him…

'You'll check…' The old man's voice was failing him now. Each word was getting more and more slurred. 'You'll check her training. I wouldn't ask you to have her if she wasn't any good, but…she's a good girl, my Tess. I ought to know. Will you check her credentials?'

'I'll check,' he said heavily, and this time Louise's glance was curious. His reluctance must be obvious.

'And if she's any good, you'll employ her?'

'I'm making no promises,' Mike told him. 'I'm not sure we need another doctor.'

'Oh, Dr Llewellyn.' Louise could no longer keep silent. The nurse was practically agog. 'Not need…? Oh, of course we need another doctor. If Dr Westcott would agree to work here…'

'Just say you'll try,' Henry begged. 'Mike… What do you say?'

He gripped Mike's hand hard, pleading—and there was nowhere left for Mike to go.

'Very well, then,' he said at last. 'If that's what Tessa

'I asked,' Tess said kindly. 'I can see I'm needed around here, Dr Llewellyn, if only to do something about Mrs Havelock's asthma.'

'Mrs Havelock's asthma is fine.'

'It's all in her head?'

'No. But she uses it—'

'As a tool. I guessed that. But what have you done about it?'

'Nothing,' he said more sharply than he'd intended. 'It's none of my business.'

'Yes, it is. Louise is depressed and I'll bet Louise is your patient, too.'

'Yes, but—'

'You don't have time to look after the psychological well-being of all your patients.' Tess nodded sympathetically and studied her toes. 'You know, I think Louise could do with gold stars. I think I'll suggest it. And tomorrow…'

'Tomorrow?' He was listening in trepidation. What next?

'Harvey Begg has asked Louise to go to the shire ball with him tomorrow night. Is Harvey an eligible young man?'

Mike blinked. Harvey… Conversation with Tessa was like holding onto an octopus, he thought, confused. You never knew which hand would grab you next. Or where you'd be led. Harvey Begg…

'I guess you could say Harvey Begg's eligible.' He managed a smile. 'Harvey's our local accountant. He's very solid, in every sense of the word. Balding. Mid-thirties. Drives a Volvo and plays cribbage.'

'Ugh.' Tessa's nose wrinkled. 'Not my cup of tea. Still…' She smiled. 'Louise seems smitten. Each to his own, I say, and maybe there's passion in cribbage that I haven't seen before. And the back seats of Volvos are huge!'

'Tess!'

She chuckled. 'Oh, well, maybe not. But Louise is getting her chance to find out tomorrow. I've arranged to mom-sit.'

'*You…*'

'Grandpa will be still in hospital.' Her face grew serious for a moment. 'I can't keep staying here, taking up a hospital room. I know that. So tomorrow night I'll stay at Louise's place—Louise's mom can think it's because Louise is doing me a favour, offering me accommodation—but it'll let Louise go to her ball. And after that…'

'After that?' Mike was eating but he was eating on automatic pilot. He felt as if he were being pushed along by a tidal wave.

'After that I'll go back out to the farm and stay there until Grandpa comes home.'

'You really are serious about staying?'

'I really am.'

Mike hesitated, not sure where to take it from here.

'And…you seriously would like a job?' he asked slowly.

Her face brightened.

'Absolutely.' Her eyes met his and there was determination behind her gaze. 'Mike, I do want to stay, but Grandpa's going to feel too guilty if I stay just to look after him. It would be much better if I could combine my medicine with his care.'

'For how long?'

'For however long it takes.'

'Tess, we could be talking years here. There's no guarantees Henry will be fit enough to look after the farm on his own again. Ever.'

'I know that.'

'So what will you do, then?'

'If you're agreeable, I'll take him back to his farm and keep him as happy as I can for the rest of his life,' she said simply. 'If I can practise medicine here, then everything falls into place. If Grandpa needs extra help, I'll be able to afford it.' She hesitated and her tongue flicked out to moisten her lips. It was a gesture of uncertainty—her first. 'If…if you'll have me.'

If he'd have her… He stared across the table at this extraordinary woman while he tried to figure out what to say. She'd burst into his life like a flash of flame and he'd felt breathless ever since. As if his world were being turned upside down.

He didn't want this girl. He didn't. In less than two days she'd destroyed the even tempo of his existence. For Mike Llewellyn, life was work. Life was medicine and dedication and caring. Life had nothing to do with painting gold stars on your toenails.

But…

But the valley was grossly medically understaffed. Maureen had been right when she'd said he was overworked. There had been times of late when Mike had been forced to cut corners—to not question as closely as he should during an examination, or to make do with changing a dressing three times a week rather than daily. And a vaccination programme should be started in earnest, and a health programme for the elderly and…

And the town needed another doctor. But not this… flibbertigibbet.

'Why don't you want me?' she asked curiously, watching his face. 'Louise tells me you need a doctor. Every nurse in this hospital— Every person I've met says the valley needs an extra doctor. Is it because I'm US-trained?'

'No.'

'Is it because I'm a woman, then?'

'No!'

'Look, I'm serious about working here,' she said firmly, her smile fading. She put her hands flat on the table and met his look. 'Mike, I'm a good doctor,' she told him. 'I know I'm trained in city medicine and there's a heap here I need to learn, but I'm willing and I want to try.'

'But...why do you want to leave the States?'

'I don't,' she said flatly. 'But, well, Mom and I have always felt dreadful about Grandpa. We felt bad that Dad wouldn't come home. Mom's always brought me up to think I was half-Australian. And this way...'

She sighed, her voice now serious. 'Mike, I've told you I'm interested in family medicine,' she said. 'That's not a lie. But in the States, well, more and more, medicine's being taken over by the specialists. As an internist I won't get to see kids or trauma or heart attacks or surgery. Family doctors can't do anything hands-on without getting sued.

'Here...here I can deliver babies and help with road trauma and counsel Louise about her love life and help old men with prostate problems. I won't just be sitting behind a desk, handing out pills and referrals.'

'But—'

'And Mom's behind me on this,' she said solidly. 'A hundred per cent. She was an only child and her parents are dead. She's always felt like Grandpa was our family and we shouldn't be so far apart. It's my guess that if I stay then she'll be over here in a flash, and that's a worry because she's bossier than me. But I do want to stay. I do. So employ me.'

'Tess...'

'Now—tomorrow morning,' she said softly, brooking no interruption. 'Louise says you have Saturday morning clinic. How about if I run it—with you watching?' Then, as he opened his mouth to protest, she held up her hands to silence him.

'No. Don't refuse. I know I won't be able to do heaps of things. I haven't a clue as to Australian rules and regulations. But I'm a fast learner, and if we give each patient the choice when they come in as to whether I can practise on them... We'll tell them my registration isn't through yet, so anything I say has to be backed up by you...'

'You have it all worked out, then.'

'Yes.' She tilted her chin, a trace of defiance colouring her voice. 'I do. Anything wrong with that?'

What could be wrong?

If someone had asked him a month ago—or even a week ago—whether he'd like a partner, he'd have jumped at the chance like a shot. He was tired past the point of exhaustion.

But a partner had always seemed an impossibility. No doctor in their right mind would practise here. The doctor who'd been here when Mike's mother died had been an alcoholic and that's why he'd ended up in such a remote place. Nowhere decent would have him.

To work here meant practising medicine at its most basic. There was no specialist back-up available. At worst, a helicopter could come in and evacuate but there was no landing strip for a light plane and in rough weather even a helicopter had trouble.

Doctors today wanted back-up and nights off and private schools for their kids. There were few opportunities in the valley for the things most doctors and their families had come to expect, and Mike knew that to attract anyone here would take a miracle.

And here was a miracle. A slim, fiery, bossy, determined miracle—with blue toes and golden stars.

So grab her and hold...

That was just what he wanted to do, he thought suddenly. That was the problem. She was sitting beside him at the big kitchen table, made to seat a staff of twelve or more. Her feet were propped up before her. Her bathrobe was vast and warm and she looked like a gift package in crimson.

She was sitting so that her gown just brushed his shoulder.

He pulled back, suddenly acutely aware of the touch, and she grinned.

'Hey, I'm not proposing to seduce you here, Dr Llewellyn,' she said mildly. 'Only work with you.' And then she furrowed her brow. 'Anyway, why so touchy? You're not gay, are you?'

'No!'

'Hmm.'

'Hmm, what?' She was watching him as if she were looking at a frog on a dissecting table, and Mike found the sensation unnerving.

'There's a problem here, but I don't know what.' She brightened. 'I'll bet you have a past.'

'A past…'

'A deep and mysterious love life of which we know not.' She grinned again. 'A skeleton in the closet. Am I right?'

'Dr Westcott…'

'Oh, I am right.' Her smile widened. 'How about I do a bit of matchmaking? If the Volvo and cribbage doesn't do the trick, how about Louise?'

'Tessa!' His voice was an explosion but for the life of him he couldn't stop a chuckle. This girl was incorrigible. And now she was smiling straight back at him.

'That's better,' she said approvingly. 'You look ever so nice when you smile.' She swung her crazy feet off the table and stood up. 'How about it, Doctor? As of tomorrow, can I be on probation, please, sir? If you think I'll make a good doctor, can I stay?'

'Tessa…'

'Just say yes,' she begged. 'Then you can go to bed, which is just where you look like you ought to be.'

He stared at her, baffled. She stared right back.

'I'll be a good little doctor,' she said meekly. 'I won't

cause any trouble, please, sir. And I'll even take your most difficult patients.'

'Tess…'

'Just say yes.'

There was no choice. He stared at her for a long, long moment, but he was too tired—too confused—too just plain baffled—to make his mind think of anything but how gorgeous she looked. How he'd like to touch that magnificent flaming hair. How he'd like to—

'Yes,' he said quickly, before his traitorous mind took him one step further. 'Fine. Starting tomorrow morning, Dr Westcott, you're on probation.'

CHAPTER FIVE

TESSA'S probation started fifteen minutes later. Mike had barely put his head on his pillow when the phone rang. It was Louise, ringing from Reception.

'Doctor, there's a fire at the hotel. Rachel from the fire brigade just rang. She needs you.'

'How bad?' Mike was suddenly wide awake, all trace of weariness gone. At the sound of his voice Strop lifted his head from his basket, cast him a reproachful glare and went straight back to sleep.

'Rachel says there are people trapped,' Louise said, her normally placid voice unsteady. 'I'll call in all staff. If you go ahead with the ambulance, I'll organise things here.'

Hell!

It took Mike all of ten seconds to haul on pants, sweater and shoes. Leaving Strop to his beauty sleep, he emerged from his apartment at the rear of the hospital in time to see the valley's second fire engine screaming past.

The ambulance officers were already backing the ambulance up to the casualty entrance.

'What'll we take, Doc?' one of them called, as they saw his shadowy figure running toward them. 'Any extras?'

'Shove in as much saline as we have in the emergency room, and soak some blankets before we go. Leave them on the floor of the van, sopping wet.'

Mike was barely awake but his mind was working lightning fast. This was his nightmare—an accident with multiple casualties where there was no medical back-up. 'Do we know what's happening?' he demanded.

'I don't think they know down there yet,' Owen, the

senior ambulance officer, told him. 'But Rachel sounded sick and you know Rachel. If she's worried then it's bad.'

'Right. Let's get down there and see.'

'I'm coming too.'

It was Tessa, slipping out of the casualty entrance to join them. She'd replaced her crimson bathrobe with black jogging pants and a crimson sweater, her hair had been hauled back in a knot and she was shoving her feet into sneakers as she ran. 'I was talking to Louise when the call came. Louise told me what's happening, and you might need me.'

Before Mike could say a word, she heaved herself up into the rear of the ambulance. She took the bags of saline from Owen and shoved them behind her, as if she'd been working with the man for years. Then she looked down into Mike's astonished face. 'Well, what are we waiting for?' she demanded.

There was no way Mike could argue. Argument took time, and if there were multiple casualties...well, he'd be grateful to have Tessa. He'd be grateful to have any medical body, he thought, Bill's words about Doris the pig echoing once more in his mind.

But suddenly, especially, he was grateful for Tess. Why did the thought of her alongside him make the thought of what lay ahead less fearful?

Tess moved aside to make room for him, and he climbed in to join her without a word. It seemed his medical partnership was about to start.

Mike was silent on the three-minute ride down to the town. The boys had the siren screaming and lights flashing so to speak would have been impossible anyway, but mentally Mike was gearing himself for what lay ahead.

It was midnight. By this time of night the pub should be closed for casual drinkers so there shouldn't be scores of trapped victims. There'd only be the guests.

The valley's hotel had seen better times as an accommodation house. Trendy bed-and-breakfast accommodation had taken over the once lucrative tourist trade. The hotel's guest rooms had become run-down and little used.

There were always one or two people using them, though. The guests now were usually men who had little choice—men who paid a few dollars for minimal accommodation and didn't expect much.

Mike was aware of Tessa's eyes on him, watching. It was as if she were reading his mind, he thought. She just watched…

No. It was as if she could see into his mind and didn't need to read. It was as if she just knew… She sat calmly on the stretcher opposite him, her hands clasped loosely in her lap as she waited for the ambulance to reach its destination.

For a fireball, she was a restful woman, Mike thought suddenly. She was making no demands on him now, and Mike sensed that she'd support him all the way here. She was acting like a true professional, and Mike felt an overwhelming surge of gratitude that she'd come.

And then the ambulance screamed around the last corner, and every other consideration but immediate need was washed away.

The hotel was well alight. The old, two-storied building hadn't been painted for years. This year's summer had been long and hot. The cooler weather of approaching winter was here now, but there'd been little rain. The building was therefore tinder-dry. Whatever had happened here—whether it had been a small spark or a larger explosive force setting things off—the flames had caught and held, and one look was enough to tell Mike that there was no way the local firefighters could save this.

And who was inside? Could anyone help them?

May there be nobody, please, God…

The whole top floor was alight and, as the ambulance screamed around the corner of the main street and the occupants of the ambulance stared in horror, the top left-hand side of the hotel roof started caving in on itself.

Dear God.

Then the ambulance was pulling in behind the fire units, careful to leave space for men and hoses between, and Mike was striding down into the noise and heat to see what he could do in all this.

He got two feet from the ambulance doors before he was caught by Rachel Briny, head of the fire team. Rachel was tiny and tough and as capable as ten men. Wherever there was trouble in the town, there was Rachel—and thank God for it.

'I've got Les Crannond over here for you, Doc. He needs seeing first.'

Mike nodded. Les was the local publican, and if Rachel said he needed to be seen first then Mike believed her.

'Burns?'

'Yeah. He's down behind the firetruck. I've got boys dousing him with water. Don't think he'll conk out on us, but his legs… Pants caught alight just as we got him out.'

'What else, Rach?'

'Nothing yet,' she said abruptly. 'Worse luck. Can't get upstairs, and upstairs is starting to come downstairs all by itself. Let you know if we find anything but don't hold your breath. Les says there're two left up there, but God help them if he's right.'

And she turned and started barking orders as she ran again to face the fire.

Mike turned to find Tess beside him, her arms full of sodden blankets and clutching Mike's bag under her load.

'Tell me where to go.'

He didn't answer, but swerved behind the truck where Rachel had said he'd find Les, leaving Tess to follow.

Les was in a mess.

The publican lay flat on the bitumen, his face grey with shock and pain. He looked as if he was about to pass out. One of the firemen was running water over his legs, and Mike saw that the cloth of his pants had burned almost away.

'Keep going, Robby,' he told the young firefighter. 'Keep that water going. The cooler you can get those legs, the less chance we'll have of having full-degree burns.'

Few people realised that even after the source of the burn was removed, flesh could keep burning. Twenty minutes continuous cooling was the rule in emergency medicine, and Mike wasn't about to break it now.

He knelt down before Les, and Tess knelt beside him. As Mike lifted Les's wrist to find his pulse—the man looked deeply shocked and cardiac arrest was a real possibility here—Tess hauled open Mike's bag.

'He has a heart condition,' Mike said brusquely. 'He had a heart attack two years ago and bypass surgery.' The burns were bad, but a heart attack was what he was most afraid of here.

'You want morphine?' Tess asked, nodding as her eyes rested on Les's face. If he had a heart condition on top of shock and these burns... Tessa's expression said she knew what they were dealing with.

'Saline, then morphine.'

'You got it.'

They worked silently and at speed, and Mike was once more overwhelmingly grateful for Tessa's presence. The two ambulance men had disappeared, no doubt leaving the major casualty to Mike and doing their own reconnaissance of what else needed doing.

That was the way they usually worked in emergencies. With only one doctor in Bellanor, it was impossible for

Mike to perform triage—the careful sorting out of priorities—in an emergency. The ambulance boys did it for him.

There was no doubt when Mike stepped back from Les they'd have more work for him, and if they thought someone needed him urgently then they'd find him soon enough. Mike was accustomed to working alone—but to have Tess beside him was a godsend.

The heat here was indescribable. No firefighter would get off unscathed, and yet they had to try. There was no way they could simply allow the hotel to burn to ash. With the hotel so close to other buildings they had to try and contain it, and contain it fast.

And there was still the possibility of more people inside.

Mike couldn't think of that. Tess was handing him a syringe. He took it, and she set up a makeshift stand for the saline while he found a vein. By the time he had the saline running, the bag was self-supporting.

He didn't have to ask Tess for what he needed next. The minute the saline was in, she had morphine ready.

Les muttered and his eyes rolled back in his head. Mike was inserting the syringe of morphine so it was Tess who lifted Les's wrist and found the pulse. She bent her face close to his so he could hear her over the roar of the flames and the shouts around them.

'It's OK, Les,' she said softly—urgently. 'It's OK. You're out of danger. The fire's being contained. Just relax. Don't fight it. We're in charge now. Not you. The painkiller will take effect in just a moment, but I don't want you to fight it. Just relax.'

Mike glanced up at her in swift surprise. She sounded so much in control…

What had he expected? He didn't know, but he now knew what he had here. Tessa sounded competent and sure and totally reassuring. She almost had Mike believing there was nothing to worry about.

'Sam…' Les moaned. 'It was Sam…'

'Is Sam Fisher inside?' Mike demanded, and Les managed a weak nod.

'Stupid bastard. I told him no radiators. I told him. But he keeps sneaking them in. Then he drinks in bed—gets himself blind drunk—gets hot and throws the covers off.'

'It's happened before.'

'Last week. He burned a bloody great hole in the floor before he woke up. I nearly chucked him out then, but he swore he wouldn't do it again.'

'Sam Fisher's an alcoholic,' Mike explained grimly to Tess. 'He often stays in the hotel. It's almost his permanent home.'

He finished administering the morphine and took Les's hand. Still the young firefighter was playing water gently over Les's legs, and Mike's eyes silently ordered Robby to continue. 'You're OK now, Les,' he told the publican. 'We have you safe. It looks like Sam might have burned himself to death, but you know as well as me that by the time Sam goes to sleep he's so far drunk he's almost paralytic. The smoke will have taken hold before he felt a thing.'

'But Hugh,' Les moaned.

'Hugh…?'

'Hugh Wade's in there. You know him, Doc. Young fella. My nephew. Getting married next Saturday to Doreen Hirrup. Lives on a farm ten miles out. Come down for the wedding rehearsal and I gave him a room free.'

Oh, no…

There was no time to take this in. There was a sudden warning shout from closer to the fire, and then a crash so loud it hurt Mike's ears. The flames reached a roaring crescendo, and there were sparks flying two hundred feet into the air. Mike looked up as the whole top storey of the place crumpled.

'Oh, God…' Les groaned beneath their hands, and his face turned even more grey.

'Mike…' Tess said warningly. If Les went into cardiac arrest here… Mike glanced up at her face and he could guess what she was thinking. She wanted her ER facilities she was used to back home in the States. She wanted a crash cart—electronic defibrillator—a cardiac specialist or six at the ready…

They had themselves plus one white-faced fireman—no more than a boy—who was trying to keep his hand steady as he sprayed the water across Les's legs. And that was all they had.

And then there was another shout behind them, different from the barked orders and shouts from the firefighters. This was a male voice, strong and full of fear, and he sounded as if he'd been running.

'Les! Les! Oh, God, Les… Has anyone seen my uncle?'

'Hugh!' Mike stood, searching the weird, flame-lit night for the source of the voice. 'Hugh!'

A long, lanky youth came stumbling toward them, his face ashen.

'Doc, it's my uncle. Have you seen him? Les… Oh, God, is he in there?'

'He's here, Hugh,' Mike said roughly, hauling the lad down so Les could see his nephew as well as Hugh see his uncle. 'He's burned his legs but he's safe.'

'Oh, hell, Les…' And the boy burst into tears.

'OK.' Mike got wearily to his feet. He'd done all he could do here for the moment. 'Can you look after this, Tess?' He motioned to Les and the boy. 'I'll see what else needs doing.'

And he slipped away into the night to seek further casualties.

It was twenty minutes before they finally loaded Les into the ambulance. In that time they'd treated six firefighters for smoke inhalation and scorched eyes. Finally, though, the great burning heap became manageable. There were no more tragedies waiting to happen here so Mike and Tess could be spared to take Les back to the hospital.

One of the ambulance men stayed back with first-aid gear, but any more casualties would surely just be minor and could either make their own way back to Casualty or be driven in a normal vehicle. There was only one more major casualty expected—and no one was expecting miracles for Sam Fisher.

Hugh came to the hospital with his uncle.

'I should 'a been there,' he said over and over again in a voice that trembled. 'My room was just next to the old codger's. I should 'a…'

The boy stared down at Les's legs. They knew now that Les had been burned trying to get up the stairs to reach his nephew.

'I didn't tell him I was going out,' Hugh muttered. 'I mean…our families are so bloody righteous. Doreen uses a sleepout at the back of her folks' place. They thought I was staying at the hotel but after they went to bed I'd sneak back, like. I mean…' His voice grew defensive. 'We are getting married next week. But then we heard the shouting and the bangs and sirens and everything and Doreen looked out and said the pub's on fire and I couldn't believe it. I came so fast…'

He stared down at his trousers. His fly was half-undone, and with a self-conscious shrug he hauled up the zipper. 'Bloody fool,' he muttered, and it was unclear who he was referring to, but his hand came down onto his uncle's shoulder. 'To try and get me out…'

'I woulda still tried to get Sam out,' Les groaned, and grabbed his nephew's hand and held it. 'Would 'a been burned anyway. Weren't your fault, Hugh. And I'll still make your wedding. You see if I don't.'

He wouldn't. Tess looked down at those charred legs and winced. Les had months of skin grafts ahead of him.

There were three solid hours of work before they could think of bed. Firstly they stabilised Les as well as they could, but there was little they could do for his legs in Bellanor. Mike organised helicopter evacuation.

'He needs a specialist burns unit,' he told a stricken Hugh. 'We don't have the facilities here to cope with burns like this. He's burned about thirty per cent of his total skin area. I'd guess about twenty-five per cent is full-thickness burns. I can't guarantee his survival if he stays here.'

There was no more to be said, but it was a subdued Hugh who, an hour later, climbed into the helicopter with his uncle and the evacuation medical team.

'Because I can't get it outa my mind that he did it for me,' he explained. 'And he don't have a wife or kids to look after him. He's only got me. I'll look after the old bugger.'

'It's probably true,' Mike said wearily, as he turned back to the queue of firefighters needing treatment—mostly for minor eye injuries. Dear God, he was tired, but there was also overwhelming sadness running through his fatigue. 'And Les knows it. I doubt if Les would have crashed through a barrier of flames just to save Sam.'

'Hey, Mike, don't think about it,' Tess said steadily, and her hand came out to touch his arm. 'What's done's done. Our job is to make the best of what's ahead.'

It was true. He gave himself a fierce mental jolt—and her hand was still on his arm. Thank God for Tessa. She made his weariness and his sadness just a little bit easier. Bad but bearable.

There was little time for any more thought after that. There was too much work. They worked side by side, washing out eyes and treating one firefighter after another for minor burns. The fire had been an inferno and the men had taken crazy risks to get Les out. By three in the morning Mike was so exhausted he could barely stand, and if Tess hadn't been there…

She was. That was all that mattered. Her presence seemed to be all that was holding him up.

'You can go to bed now,' he told her, as the last of their patients disappeared back out into the night. The hotel was now nothing but a vast pile of smouldering ash. Somewhere inside was what remained of Sam Fisher, but Sam had built his own funeral pyre. There was little hope of finding anything recognisable.

But Tess was watching him closely, and she shook her head.

'No.'

'No?'

'You're exhausted,' she said softly. 'But me… I slept most of the afternoon. I'm still bright-eyed and bushy-tailed and ready to go.' Then her voice softened. 'And I haven't just lost someone I was fond of in a fire.'

Mike's eyes flew to hers.

'How—?'

'How do I know? I can tell the signs,' she said gently. 'You're quiet. You're too quiet for someone who isn't feeling pain.'

'I…'

'Want to tell me about Sam?'

He didn't. Or…did he?

'Sam was…just a patient,' he said.

'And?'

'He's old and fragile and he feels…he felt the cold.' Mike's gaze turned inwards, remembering. 'Sure, he's a drunk, but he's a likeable old drunk. I had him down for a nursing-home bed but we never have any spare when he's in the mood for coming and when I do have a spare bed then he's feeling independent and obstinate and tells me I'm fussing. Maybe I should have fussed more...'

'You can't force people to do what they don't want to.'

'No.' He stared bleakly into the middle distance and then shook his head. 'Anyway, if Sam hasn't drunk all his pension cheque, he stays in the pub. And Les is lousy with the bedding. The hotel has...had south-facing windows and it's an old, old building.

'It's April now and the nights are turning frosty. I organised Sam more blankets, but it's my guess he sold them. A decent blanket will fetch you fifty dollars. Fifty dollars equals ten bottles of cheap plonk. A cheap radiator costs you ten.'

'Oh, Mike...'

'I should have gone to see Les before this happened,' he said harshly. 'Hell, I should have seen it coming. Last time he was in to see me...only three days ago...Sam was complaining of chilblains. He's so damned thin, he has no body fat to keep him warm. He *had* no body fat...'

'Mike...'

She took two steps forward and lifted his hand in hers. She cupped it between her fingers and her gaze met his and held.

'Mike, don't do this to yourself.'

'Don't do what?' The feel of her hand was making things even more surrealistic. It was as if he were in a bad dream. Floating.

'You're exhausted,' she said softly. 'Go to bed.'

Bed. Ha! How could he go to bed?

'The ambulance boys are still working. There'll be more people to see before morning.'

'I can see them,' she told him.

'You're not—'

'Not registered to work here?' She drew herself up to

her full five feet six inches and glared. 'No, I'm not. But I'll tell you what, Dr Llewellyn. I'd rather be treated by me, an unregistered doctor, than by you, a doctor who's past his sleep-by date. You should be stamped, "This doctor has not slept the requisite number of hours in the past twenty-four." Truck drivers in the States have a system like that, so I'm introducing it here. Now. Consider yourself stamped, Dr Llewellyn. Go to bed.'

'I can't.'

'Go!' She put her hands on his shoulders and shoved, a crimson powerhouse, propelling him out into the corridor. Before he knew what she was about, he was on the other side of the door. 'Go on. Go. I'll bet your dog's asleep. You go and join him. Unless you think I'm incapable—which I'm not. If I want to do anything really hard, like the odd spot of neurosurgery, I'll call you. I promise.'

'Tess...'

She softened then and smiled up at him, and her smile made his insides feel really strange. Weird.

'OK. I'll call you for things a bit less complicated than neurosurgery. For anything I can be sued over if I muck up, I'll call you. I promise. But go to bed. Please, Mike.'

Her hands were still on his shoulders. He stared down at her and the twisting sensation in his gut got stronger and stronger. What was happening here?

He didn't have a clue. What mattered though... Hell, she was right. If he didn't sleep now he'd fall right over. It must be sleeplessness that was making him feel so strange.

What else?

'OK,' he said finally—flatly—and his voice came out not as he'd expected. His voice sounded devoid of any emotion—and that was the opposite of what he was feeling. But he knew he couldn't stay standing here one minute longer. 'OK, Dr Westcott. I'll go to bed.'

And somehow he managed to haul himself away from

her hands. Somehow he made himself turn around and face the other way and take the few long steps to the bend in the corridor.

When all he wanted to do… All he wanted to do was to gather her into his arms and kiss her.

CHAPTER SIX

MIKE slept until eleven the next morning. He opened his eyes and stared at his clock—and then sat bolt upright. What the hell...?

He swung out of bed, and then paused as a knock resounded on the outer door of his apartment. That must have been what had woken him. He dived under the sheet again, and two seconds later his bedroom door swung wide and Tessa's face peeped around. When she saw he was awake, she beamed.

'Well, good morning.'

He could only stare. A rejoinder just wouldn't come out. Tess was dressed all in white, like a super-efficient little medico. She had on a white lab coat over white pants and T-shirt, white sneakers and a big white ribbon was hauling back that riot of red hair.

'You like my bridal outfit?' She whirled, a tray in hand, for him to inspect.

He did. He did very much. She looked just great!

She also smelled great. She stopped whirling and walked across the room to deposit her tray on his bedside table. The tray held fried eggs and bacon, toast and strong black coffee. It seemed an age since supper last night and the smell was just wonderful.

'Here's your breakfast,' she said cheerfully. 'I left it as long as I could, but any later and it'd have to be lunch. And that's the last egg you're allowed this week, Dr Llewellyn. If you're not worried about your cholesterol then you should be, and as your new medical partner I feel I have to make a stand.'

'But…' He stared up at the girl above him, and then he stared at his alarm clock. It must have stopped working. He'd set it for six.

'I turned it off,' Tess said, seeing where he was looking. She smiled benignly, for all the world as if she'd done him a favour.

'You—'

'I sneaked in to check you were asleep about five a.m,' she told him blithely. 'Didn't see me, huh? I'm a born sneak. And as for Strop! What a watchdog! He snored and rolled over and that's the only peep I heard out of him. When I opened the door just now, he took one whiff of the bacon and headed for the kitchen at what I can only suppose is what he thinks is a run. Good grief!'

'But the clock…' Mike reached to lift the plate of eggs and bacon—and then thought better of it. He made a self-conscious grab at the sheet. Hell, why on earth didn't he wear pyjamas?

But Tess either didn't notice or wasn't fussed at him presenting his nakedness from the hips up. 'Yeah. The clock. I saw what time you'd set it for,' she told him. 'Six a.m.! What sort of a crazy time is that? I turned it off.' Her smile widened. 'Aren't you glad I did?'

'No,' he said tersely, hauling his scattered wits together and the sheet higher. 'I'm not. I have surgery. Saturday morning's always frantic.'

'I disagree.'

'What do you mean—you disagree?'

'I just did your surgery,' she said. 'That's why I'm dressed like this—as opposed to you being dressed like you are. Very informal, I must say.' Then, as colour started mounting under his tan, she kept right on going. 'I figured I had to make a nice efficient impression first off—before everyone gets to know the real me. And it wasn't frantic at all. It was great fun. I've met the nicest bunch of people.'

She grinned down at his confusion. 'Mind you, I may have prescribed wart medicine for angina, or vice versa.'

'You're kidding,' he said faintly, and she took pity on him and chuckled.

'Yep. I'm kidding. I'm pretty sure I got everything right. Maureen—your nurse-receptionist—is just the greatest. She sat in with me and we had a copy of *MIMS*, which told us the brand names for the generic medicines, so I don't think we've messed anything up. Maureen rang Ralph, the pharmacist, and you're to pop in this afternoon and countersign everything. That'll cover the legalities. But we did just fine.'

'What…?' He shook his head, trying to wake up. This felt just like a dream. 'What have you seen? Who…?'

'Lots of things.' Tess hauled a chair from by the door and sat down beside him. 'Lots of people. Eat your breakfast. It's getting cold.' She lifted the coffee-jug and poured two cups, one for Mike and one for her, then settled back like a visitor in a long-term hospital, here for the duration. Mike's sense of unreality grew even stronger.

'I saw Mrs Dingle's arthritic knee,' she told him—as though she'd really enjoyed the sensation. 'I took out Susie Hearn's stitches. I listened to Bert Sharey's wheezy chest and his problems with his best heifer, and I gave him antibiotics and a lecture about smoking too much. I told Caroline Robertson she was pregnant, and then I had to tell her husband because they've been trying so long they didn't believe me…'

'Caroline Robertson's pregnant?'

'She's about three months, I'd say,' she said serenely. 'It made me feel good to tell them. They're very happy.'

'You're kidding.' Mike shook his head. 'Tess, do you know how important this is? If you've made a mistake…'

'I don't mistake pregnancy at three months.' Tess appeared miffed. 'I agree that some things might be different between Australians and Americans—like their nasal twang and the things they do to peanut butter—but pregnancy shouldn't be included. I did a full examination and everything's fine.'

'But...' Mike shook his head again in sheer disbelief. 'The Robertsons have tried every treatment known to man, and then some. In January they finally stopped trying and applied for adoption.'

'They can't have stopped trying entirely.' She grinned again, and then appeared once more to concentrate. 'Who else? I can't think. There were heaps of patients booked in. I've left all their cards out so you can see who I've seen and what I've done.'

'And...the patients in hospital? They need—' Mike was practically flabbergasted.

'I've seen them, too,' she said blithely. 'I let Mrs Pritchard go home because she told me you'd promised she could today, and I couldn't see any reason to keep her longer. I decided to keep Hal Connor's drip in. It packed up about five a.m—that was when I checked on you—but I still think he needs the fluids.' She paused. 'Oh, and Grandpa—'

'He's OK?'

'Yes. His electrolytes are almost back to normal and there's nerve function all along the affected side. And he's loving me working here.' She smiled her pleasure. 'Which makes two of us. Me and him. So, how about you, Dr Llewellyn? Are you happy to have me working here?'

'I don't seem to have a choice,' he said slowly, munching into toast without thinking. God, this felt good. Weird but good. To have a long sleep followed by breakfast...

The grey weight of exhaustion he'd been carrying had slipped from him and he felt ten years younger. He was confused, but at least now he wasn't bone-weary. 'Is there anything you haven't done?'

'I don't think so.'

'What about what's happening at the hotel?'

Tessa's smile faded. 'Yeah, well... Everything can't be good. But there's news from Melbourne. Les is settled at the burns unit at the Alfred. He has a long road ahead of him but his condition didn't deteriorate through the trip.'

'But?' Mike could tell here was something else. Tessa's bright face had clouded.

'I went down to what's left of the hotel at about seven this morning. They were pulling... Well, they were pulling what may be the remains of Sam's body from the ashes. I've identified it as human remains and it was hard enough to do that. I've organised for him to be brought into the mortuary, but the formal identification...' She shrugged. 'I'm afraid that might have to be up to you, Mike. You'll need dental records. Medical records... I don't know. I would have spared you that, but—'

'Hell, you've done enough.'

'No.' Tess shook her head. 'I haven't done nearly enough.' She clasped her hands with the same restfulness he'd seen the night before on the ambulance trip to the fire, and her face grew earnest.

'Mike, the more I see, the more I know this is my sort of medicine,' she said seriously. 'In the States, medicine's so specialised. Even if I choose to do family medicine, I won't get to see anything like I saw this morning. I won't get to see surgery or gynaecology or trauma. But here I see so much. In one short morning I've seen it all.'

'It can be pretty mind-deadening,' he told her flatly. 'And it can be frightening. And sometimes it can be both. You're coping with coughs and colds and people's personal problems and life-threatening trauma all in the same day...'

She bit her lip and thought this through, and when she nodded he knew she was sure. 'I know. I know it can be dreadful and I know it can be dreary,' she said finally. 'But this is what I want. Probation or not, I want to work here, Mike. Regardless of Grandpa. This is where I want to be.'

'Tessa...' He stared at her, troubled. He didn't know the first thing about this woman. She seemed so sure, but he wasn't sure at all. All he did know of this woman scared him stupid.

'I'm rushing you,' she said softly, standing up again. 'Finish your breakfast, have another cup of coffee and think about it. You're on call for the hospital for the next couple of hours. That's another reason I'm waking you now. I've been invited to a football match this afternoon, and before that I'm off to do an obstetrician's house call.'

'An obstetrician's...'

'To Doris the pig,' she said cheerfully. 'Doris should be up to receiving visitors by now. I'm taking the Polaroid to get baby snaps for Grandpa. I'll pass on your regards, shall I?'

'Tess...'

'Of course I shall,' she said warmly. 'After your help in delivering all those babies, it'd surprise me if Doris hasn't named one of her sons Mike.'

She left him to his breakfast, and she left him feeling as stunned as he'd ever felt in his life before.

The day passed in a dream.

For the first time in Mike couldn't remember how long, he had little to do. He checked Tessa's medical records and found nothing to complain of. She'd been thorough and competent and careful, and there was nothing that he wouldn't have done himself. Baffled, he took Strop for a stroll down to the pharmacy to countersign Tessa's prescriptions.

'Your new partner's a damned fine girl,' Ralph, the town's pharmacist, told him. 'Our Wendy went in this morning all stirred up because her periods are irregular.

She's getting 'em every two months and she jumped at the chance of seeing a lady doctor.

'Well, she's come home happy as a lark. Dr Westcott told her she'd have to be the luckiest fourteen-year-old girl in the district to get a period only every two months. It's what her mother's been telling her over and over, but do you think Wendy'd listen? But your Dr Westcott did the trick.'

The pharmacist sighed and dug his hands deep into the pockets of his white coat. 'A woman doctor,' he said in satisfaction. 'That's what this place needs. Plus…' He grinned. 'I can read her handwriting. A woman doctor with legible handwriting. Make her sign on the dotted line this minute.'

Yeah, right…

Mike came out of the pharmacy still troubled by a sense of unreality. This wasn't happening.

There were the sound of car hooters from down by the river and he glanced at his watch. It was mid-afternoon. The local football game would be in full swing.

Football… 'I've been invited to a football match,' Tess had said.

He paused in indecision. He had his mobile phone on his belt. The locals played rough and there were always one or two minor injuries, so any minute now the phone would buzz into life.

He didn't want to go back to the surgery.

'I've been invited to a football match…'

'What do you reckon, Strop? Do you feel like a football match?'

So Mike strolled the two blocks to the football field, telling himself all the time it was just to save the players the trouble of coming to the surgery. Not that he believed it for a minute.

The football competition here was a low-key, Australian

Rules game. The ground had been marked out on the river flat, which meant whenever the river rose the games had to be cancelled. Four white posts were stuck in at each end of a roughly painted oval, and a players' tent had been erected for each team. There was also a beer and pie tent. That was it. As a stadium it left a bit to be desired, but what the locals lacked in facilities they made up for in enthusiasm.

There were cars parked all around the playing field. Saturday afternoon football here was a town ritual. The women watched from the cars, with Thermos flasks and picnic baskets wedged between them on the front seats. Many had travelled in from outlying farms, and this was their social contact for the week. The only way anyone knew they were watching football was when a goal was scored. Then the hooters blared out from every second car in the place.

The men were made of sterner stuff, though, than to stay in the cars. They didn't need the warmth—they left that to the women. Bellanor's male population spent the game clustered around the beer tent—a hundred or so males spread no further than carting distance for the next round.

The rest of the boundary was left to the kids and the teenagers.

First off, Mike released Strop from his lead. From past experience, Strop would either spend the match hauling Mike's arm off, trying to reach the pie tent, or he'd spend the match staring soulfully at pie tent customers, so as far as Mike could figure there was no choice. 'Don't eat too much,' he told Strop. 'Any more than one pie and you're out of the car for a week.'

Strop gave his tail a majestic wave and departed at a waddle.

Strop-less, Mike made his way slowly around the ground toward the training tents. This was where he'd be needed, he told himself, trying hard not to keep a weather eye out for Tess.

But somehow he found her. Tess was right in the middle of a huddle of teenagers. And what she was wearing… It was just plain extraordinary.

Or maybe it wasn't plain at all. Tess wore bright purple leggings, a brilliant yellow jacket and a purple cap with a yellow pompom. Oh, and purple Doc Martens on her feet for good measure.

He blinked. The colours of the teams on the ground were red and black stripes and black and white stripes respectively so, in this sea of red and black and white, Tess stood out like a sore thumb.

She was sublimely oblivious. Tessa was perched on the bonnet of Alf Sarret's FJ Holden. Alf was a nineteen-year-old car fanatic who polished his car twice a day and wouldn't let anyone look sideways at it much less sit on it, but Tessa was definitely sitting on it and she was talking and laughing as if she was nineteen years old and had known these kids all her life.

She saw him from ten yards away and a brilliant purple arm shot upwards in a wave.

'Mike. Come over here. Isn't this the craziest game? The kids have been teaching me the rules—or rather trying to teach me the rules. I think you need to be a third-generation Australian to understand them. Why aren't you wearing team colours? And who are we barracking for?'

'Who are we…?'

'The kids say I need to choose, and I need to choose now,' she said. 'Apparently I can't stay in this town without swearing allegiance to a Bellanor football club. The only trouble is—do I swear allegiance to Bellanor South Football Club or Bellanor North Football Club?' She looked around at her crowd of bemused teenagers. 'The camp here appears to be evenly divided,' she said. 'And I know Grandpa hates football. So I figure...if you and I intend to be partners then I'd better barrack for who you barrack for.' She grinned. 'The kids say otherwise we'll fight.'

If you and I intend to be partners...

He thought fleetingly of what he'd always imagined a partner might be. He'd thought of a sober, conscientious middle-aged doctor with whom he could share the load. Not this...this...this pompommed purple and yellow apparition!

'Jancourt,' he said faintly. It was all he could think of to say, and the word was met by a howl of derision from the teenagers.

'Yeah?' Tessa wasn't put off by the teenagers' reaction. Her eyes rested on Mike's face and she twinkled down at him. She dug her hands deep into the pockets of her extraordinary yellow jacket and nodded. 'OK. If you say so, Mike, then I'll barrack for Jancourt. Tell me about our team.'

'But Jancourt's hopeless,' Alf interrupted. He had nobly allowed Tess to sit on his car and was now acting as if he was in charge of her. 'Don't do it, Doc. Jancourt's the lousiest team. They lose every week.'

'Jancourt's more a name than a place,' Mike agreed. 'It's all they can do to scratch eighteen men. In fact, sometimes they play with up to half a dozen men short, and their back line has an average age of about sixty.'

'It sounds just my sort of team,' Tessa said with aplomb, and Mike grinned.

'It is,' he told her. 'If you barrack for North or South Bellanor, then every Monday morning you'll be looked at by half the population as if it's all your fault that they're feeling ill. If you barrack for Jancourt...well, every Monday morning all you'll get is sympathy.'

'Very wise.' Tess seemed perfectly satisfied with the logic. 'And what are our colours?'

'Sorry, Tessa. Not purple and yellow.'

'Rats. These are the colours of my very favourite football team at home. The Vikings.'

'They're a bit loud,' Mike said faintly, and Tessa's smile widened.

'Loud! You want loud? The true Vikings uniform has a hat with horns! Or I could be a fan of the Green Bay Packers. My mom follows the Green Bay Packers and she gets to wear cheese on her head. This is sedate in comparison.'

'Cheese?' Tess had the whole bunch of teenagers riveted to their conversation, and Tessa was revelling in it.

'I kid you not.' She chuckled. 'I swear. Green Bay Packer fans wear vast slabs of cheese on their heads—don't ask me why. The Vikings are a sensible, sane football team that a sensible, sane girl like me can follow with pride. I'll follow them to the death—I'll even wear horns—but when football clubs expect their fans to wear cheeses and a girl's mother says she's being undutiful by changing to the Vikings, well, it's enough to make a girl migrate all the way to Australia.'

'I expect it is,' Mike managed faintly.

'So what are the Jancourt team colours?' she demanded.

'Cream and brown.'

'Ugh.' Tessa's pert nose wrinkled in distaste. Then she shrugged. 'Never mind. I love purple and yellow, but I can't have everything.' Her smile returned in full and Mike could only stare.

Tess looked totally, perfectly happy. She looked as if she'd lived here all her life, and as if there was nothing more she could ask of life than to sit in a cold wind on a teenage boy's ancient jalopy and cheer a football game where she didn't even understand the rules.

She'd fit into this valley as if she'd been born here, Mike thought, wondering. In one half of one football game, Tess had managed to woo and win the town's teenage population. The group Tess was in made up the most popular kids in town and there were more teenagers sidling up to the edges of the group every minute. By tomorrow, the word would be around town that there was a new lady doctor in town and she was great!

'Oh, hell...'

There was a sudden howl from the crowd. A tackle had brought one of the forwards down, and the injured player was clutching his knee in agony out on the field.

Mike sighed and dragged his attention from Tess. 'Well, there goes my quiet time,' he said with resignation. 'I'll leave you to your friends, Dr Westcott.'

'Hey, I'm coming too.' She slid off the car and tucked her arm into his. 'I'm your partner, OK?' Her smile widened. 'I've always dreamed of running onto the field as team doctor. It's one of my career goals. Like at the movies when they interrupt with, "Is there a doctor in the house?".' They did it all the time before I graduated, but never since.'

'Well, I'm sorry to disappoint you, but I'm not running onto any ground,' he told her firmly, watching as the trainers raced over to the injured player with a stretcher at the ready.

'I'll only go if they yell that he's stopped breathing. Even then I'll wait until he turns blue. The players here have a nasty habit of getting on with the game, regardless. The only thing they ever stop for is Strop and that's because he eats the ball. It took me months to teach him the pie tent was a better place to hang out than the centre of the playing field.'

'You're kidding.' Tessa's face creased in laughter. 'It's not a good doctor image—to have a ball-eating dog.'

'No,' Mike said darkly. 'If I had my time again...'

'You'd have him put down?'

'Well...'

Tess chuckled and tucked her arm tighter in his. 'Yeah, I know. Tough he-man Dr Llewellyn—with the squishy edges. So we're not running out on the ground?'

'Last time I went onto the ground I got hit in the face with the ball.' Mike was incredibly aware of her proprietary arm. It made him feel as if every nerve in his body were alight—but, then, it'd seem churlish to haul it away. 'The player only had a bruised knee, but I copped a bloody nose and a black eye,' he managed. 'They had to help me off!'

'It's not a good professional look.' Tessa chuckled. She walked easily beside him, her arm still tucked in his. 'So where do we do our doctoring?' she asked.

'The red tent. The player who's coming off is wearing red for Bellanor North.'

'Oh. Right. I'll remember that.'

She would, too, he thought. Tessa's quick, intelligent mind was busy tucking in item after item of what she'd term useful information. You wouldn't need to tell her anything twice.

'I don't think you're supposed to come into the training tent,' he said faintly. 'The rules are rigid. Women aren't allowed.'

'Oh, pooh,' she said blithely. 'I'm not a woman here, Dr Llewellyn. I'm a doctor.' And she glanced up at him sideways and twinkled. 'Do you reckon that's something you can remember? It seems to me that it's really important.'

And what the hell was he to make of that?

Jason Keeling was clutching his leg in agony. By the time they reached him, the trainers had deposited him on the bench and were looking down helplessly. Jason wasn't letting them near his leg. He was curled almost into a foetal position, hanging onto his leg for dear life and swearing as if his life depended on it.

'OK, Jason, let's have a look,' Mike said, bending over him and trying to see.

Jason didn't look up. He was whimpering in pain and the swearing didn't ease one bit.

'Hey, I don't know half those words.'

It was Tess. Of course it was Tess. She stood back from Jason and regarded him with frank admiration, and Jason was so stunned to hear a woman in the training room that momentarily he forgot to swear. He looked up from his leg and uncurled a bit.

'Who the hell are you?' he demanded.

'I'm one half of the Bellanor medical team,' she said blithely. 'The better half. Show us your leg, Jason.'

And Jason was so flabbergasted that his hands fell away from his leg. Mike was in there before he could put them back, holding his leg and gently easing it to an extended position.

'Fancy this happening just as you were winning,' Tess said sympathetically. She perched on the end of the bench and put a sympathetic hand on his cheek. Mike could only bless her. For all Jason Keeling was six feet six inches of pure beef, he was a real wimp when it came to pain. Now, though, Tess had his full attention and Mike could run his hands carefully over the injured limb.

He couldn't feel a break…

'What do you mean—one half of the Bellanor medical team?' Jason demanded. The team trainers were staring at Tess as if she'd just flown in from Mars, and so was Jason. Mike might just as well not have been present.

'I'm a doctor.' She chuckled as she glanced around at the men's astounded expressions. 'Believe it or not, that's what I am. Mike said I might have to prove my qualifications or you'll throw me out of the training tent.'

'You can stay in any training tent you want, miss,' one of the trainers breathed. 'And I'll personally chuck out anyone who says different.'

'That's really nice of you.' Tessa's eyes danced as she twisted to look down at the injured leg. Still her hand rested on Jason's face. She was sitting so close to him that her crazy yellow jacket was brushing his body, and Jason was clearly completely thrown by the sensation. 'What's the damage, Dr Llewellyn?' she asked. 'Do you think we need to amputate? Do I get to hold him down while you chop it off?'

'I reckon we might manage without amputation.' Mike grinned in return. To examine Jason when he was in pain was usually a nightmare, but she had Jason absolutely silenced. Now she shifted from the bench to support Jason's leg as Mike carefully ran his hands from the knee down. He watched Jason's face as he did, but Jason didn't utter a whimper. 'What happened, Jason?'

'I was running,' Jason muttered. 'I just felt something...like a bang. Like something snapped.' Jason's eyes were still on Tessa, fascinated.

Mike nodded, moving to feel above the ankle. His suspicions were being confirmed here. There was a definite notching.

'Can you move your ankle, Jason? Will your toes lift?'

Jason stared wildly from Tessa to Mike, trying to collect his wits. It was as if he was having trouble remembering he had a leg at all. Tessa's pompoms and her gorgeous red hair had him in thrall. Finally he shook his head. 'Nah...' Then his face creased again as he remembered his wimpishness and he remembered his pain.

'I reckon we might get some morphine on board,' Mike told him hastily. 'That'll ease the pain.'

'But what's wrong? What's wrong?'

'I think you've torn your Achilles tendon. It's hard to

say whether it's a complete tear or not without a fuller examination, but that's what it feels like.'

'Aw, hell…'

'Hey, it beats a compound fracture,' Tessa told him. Mike was settling the leg back on the bench. Tessa turned to touch Jason lightly again on the face, and Jason stared up at her in stupefaction. 'It's not much better, I guess,' she said sympathetically, 'but a little.'

'But it'll mean I miss the rest of the season,' Jason wailed. 'I'll have to stay on the sidelines and watch…'

'Like me,' Tessa said cheerfully. 'I know nothing about this game. Back home in the States, I love football. Here, though, it sure looks different. I need someone who knows it inside out to teach me what's happening. You look like just the man—that is, if you don't mind me barracking for Jancourt.'

'Jancourt…' Jason lay back on the bench and stared up at her in stupefaction. 'Jancourt. Why the hell are you barracking for Jancourt?'

'Dr Llewellyn said I should,' Tessa said blithely. 'And he's my boss now. It's always wise to do what your boss says—don't you think?'

'Yeah. Right.' Jason couldn't think of a single thing more to say.

And neither could Mike.

There was only one more medical case for the afternoon—a bruised hamstring muscle that could be left safely in the hands of the trainers—so they got to watch most of the game. Jason was sent to the hospital. He'd need to be checked later and the leg properly X-rayed and examined, but before that the nurses could clean away the worst of the mud and his family could fuss and generally settle him down. There wasn't much more to be done in the short term.

'What if it's a complete tear?' Tessa asked as they sat on the trainers' seats and watched the Bellanor North players storm their way to victory.

'We'll send him to Melbourne.'

'There's no one closer to do orthopaedic surgery?' If the Achilles tendon was completely separated then it would have to be surgically joined. A partial tear would heal itself, given several weeks' immobilisation in plaster, but a full tear wasn't quite as easy.

'I could do it,' Mike said heavily. He was feeling really odd, sitting beside this girl. She was acting as if they'd known each other for ever—as if they were partners in every sense of the word. And yet…

Hell, he felt strange.

'You've done surgical training?' she asked.

'I trained for this job,' he told her. 'I knew I'd be isolated when I came to work here so I got myself training in everything I could get my hands on. There's not a lot of emergency medicine I can't do, but I've found it's not a lot of use if I don't have an anaesthetist.'

'I can give an anaesthetic.'

'You…'

'Now don't say it like I'm a porriwiggle,' she begged. 'The fact that I'm American doesn't mean I'm low-life. I'm not even wearing a cheese hat.' She swung her head to prove it, and her crazy purple pompoms bounced.

She wouldn't need to give an anaesthetic, Mike thought. She only had to wiggle her pompoms and she had a man mesmerised. She could do anything she wanted…

'Look, it doesn't matter whether you can give an anaesthetic or not,' he managed. 'You're not registered. You can't.'

'But Maureen says she'll swing my registration within twenty-four hours from the medical board opening for business on Monday. Jason's surgery's not urgent. We could do it Tuesday.'

'What sort of anaesthetic work have you done?' he asked. Hell, he was fascinated. He was trying to listen—not watch.

'General.' Once more, the pompom waggled. 'I told you, I've always fancied the idea of moving to the country. I was thinking I might do ER in a smaller country hospital so I figured anaesthetics—you know, intubation and pain relief and the rest—might give me an edge.

'Then I sort of changed my mind. I wanted kids and dogs and prostates instead of car smashes and drug overdoses. But I've done a solid basic training in anaesthetics. I'm not volunteering to give the anaesthetic for open heart surgery here, but I can certainly give a healthy hunk of beef like Jason a guaranteed sleep.'

Mike fell silent. He stared out over the football ground, his mind racing. What on earth…? An anaesthetist, right on his patch…

'Look, I'm not asking you to take me on trust here,' Tessa said, mistaking his expression. 'Ring my ex-boss on Monday and run through my credentials with him. Don't take me at face value. I wouldn't myself.' Then she grimaced as the phone on Mike's belt rang. 'Ugh.'

That was what Mike felt. He didn't want more work now. Or did he? Maybe he did need an excuse to leave and think things through.

The game was just coming to an end. The siren blared and the field erupted into red and black madness. A hundred car horns hooted. Mike turned away and covered his exposed ear while he talked into the phone.

By the time he'd finished, Tessa was clapping the jubilant players off the field, for all the world as if it was grand final day, she totally understood the game she'd been watching and she'd been supporting these players for years.

To Mike's bemusement, when the losing side ran off the field she greeted them with just the same enthusiasm.

As Mike came up behind her, she turned and grinned at him.

'OK. I've clapped till my hands are sore. Was that another call? Do we need to go?'

'I need to go.' It wasn't that he didn't want Tessa beside him, he thought. He figured it was just that he needed to get away for a while. He badly needed time to think. 'Stan Harper's a sixty-year-old farmer who lives out the other side of Jancourt,' he told her. 'He rang to say he's having chest pain.'

'Yeah?' Her smile faded. 'Heart?'

'In a way.' He smiled a trifle bleakly and shook his head. 'Stan's wife died six months ago. Since then he gets chest pain every few weeks or so, and he panics. I've run the gamut of tests on him and there's nothing wrong.'

'But you'll go anyway.' Tessa's face softened.

'Yeah, well…' He could get Stan to drive himself in to the hospital. It'd be safe enough. But he knew what Stan really wanted.

Stan wanted Mike to care about him a bit—to fuss like his Cathy had and to tell him he wasn't alone in the world. He wanted someone to share a beer and stare at a few cows and talk about the outcome of a football match that Stan wasn't ready to face without Cathy.

'Yeah, I'll go, but I do need to go by myself. Sorry.' He bit his lip at the sound of the words. He sounded surly.

How else was he supposed to sound? He didn't know. He needed to figure out some way to get things on a solid, sensible footing here, he decided. Maybe he needed to talk to this girl for a while. Yeah. That was it. He needed to know all about her medical training, and he needed to know soon, before he made a decision about sending Jason away for surgery.

'Tess, I should be back in town by about seven,' he said slowly, thinking his mental diary through. He wasn't expected at the shire ball until nine. There was time to talk first, especially if they did it over a meal. 'There's some steak in my refrigerator. I'm going out to the shire ball later but, well, we could eat first. Talk about things...'

'I'd love that.' She beamed and the thing was settled before he had a chance to say another word—or before he had a chance to decide whether he was totally stupid or not.

'I'll meet you in your apartment at seven,' she said. 'Unless you need me beforehand. Meanwhile, I'll stay here and celebrate or commiserate, and then I'll go and sit with Grandpa a while. But I'll be there at seven, Mike. Steak sounds fantastic.'

Hell! He felt like he was being steamrollered here, but there was little he could do about it. And maybe...maybe it was what he wanted. 'I just...need to collect Strop,' he said weakly. 'He's over at the pie tent.'

'Of course he's over at the pie tent.' Tess grinned. 'I should have known Strop would be here and where Strop would be while he was here. Don't worry about him. I'll take him home.'

'Are you sure?'

'Absolutely. It would be my very great pleasure to take care of your dog, Dr Llewellyn.'

And, as he moved away, Mike swore he heard a faint echo.

'And it would be my very great pleasure to take care of you.'

Surely he must have been mistaken!

As he'd thought, there was nothing the matter with Stan Harper.

Mike gave him a thorough once-over, but his vital signs

were all just as a healthy sixty-year-old's should be. Stan accepted the verdict with resignation—hell, it was almost as if the man wanted a heart attack—and poured him a beer. They went out to sit on the back verandah to drink it in what was almost becoming a ritual.

'I missed you at the game,' Mike told him, staring out over the mountains at the setting sun. 'Your team lost. They don't play the same without you holding up the bar and cheering for them.'

'Or Cathy hooting for all she's worth in the car,' Stan said morosely. 'I know we never stayed together at the footy, but she was always *there*. I don't know, Doc. It doesn't seem the same without her. Nothing's the same.'

There was nothing to say to that. Mike took a swig of beer and stared some more out over the paddocks. This was all he could do for this man. To be here. To be a mate.

'Why the hell don't you get married?' Stan demanded suddenly. He filled his glass again and turned his attention full on Mike. 'A man's a fool if he doesn't get married.'

'Everyone's different.'

'Yeah, but you're not a natural loner. You could do with a good woman.' Stan eyed Mike with speculation in his eyes. 'Your mum was a bonzer woman.'

'Maybe that's why I don't get married,' Mike said uneasily. 'No one measures up.'

'There's good women around. Your mum. My Cathy. You just gotta look.' Stan frowned into his glass, deep in thought.

At one level Mike welcomed this conversation. It made him uncomfortable, but at least Stan was thinking about something other than his misery.

'What about this new lady doctor?' Stan said, and all of a sudden the conversation was totally unwelcome.

'What about her?'

'They say she's a knockout.'

Mike thought of the purple pompoms and could only agree.

'How about it, Doc?' Stan demanded. 'Are you interested?'

'No.'

'Why not?'

'I'm too busy to be thinking about a love life.'

'Then think about this girl instead,' Stan said warmly. 'Not a love life. A future. A lady doctor as a wife... That'd mean half the workload and someone warm beside you in bed at night. A man'd be a fool to look a gift horse like that in the mouth.'

'Yeah. A man'd be a fool.'

A man was a fool anyway.

CHAPTER SEVEN

MIKE was late for dinner, but Tess didn't wait for him. He arrived back at the hospital to find Tess had taken dinner into her own hands. He opened his apartment door, and there she was.

'What are you doing here?' He stopped dead at the door, his nose wrinkling in automatic appreciation of the smells wafting toward him.

'You asked me to dinner—remember?' She glanced at her wrist. 'Half an hour ago. Strop and I had the choice of sitting on the doorstep and looking bereft, or taking some action. And looking bereft isn't our style.'

'I can see that,' he said faintly. Bereft? She looked anything but bereft. 'That's a great outfit!'

She looked down and grinned. She was wearing a soft white frock, but had covered it with a green theatre gown from the hospital linen supply.

On someone else it might have looked ridiculous. It didn't look the least bit ridiculous on Tess.

'You don't have an apron,' she said accusingly. She looked around the flat. 'In fact, you don't seem to have a lot, Dr Llewellyn. Do you believe in a nice, spartan existence?'

'It's what I like.' Holy heck, he was out of his depth here.

'But you like your dog?' Someone—it must have been Tess—must have fed Strop, or maybe he'd eaten one pie too many to appreciate the smells Tess was conjuring up. He was lying full length under the table, gently snoring. Now Tess motioned out the window, towards one truly magnificent, hand-built doghouse. It was about four feet in length, painted in gold and red, with magnificent Greek lettering across the front.

'''Stropacropolis''.'

'You built that?' Tess asked, awed.

'He had a broken hip when I got him,' Mike said weakly. 'It was the least I could do.'

'And, like Jacob, you always do the least you can do. I can see that about you.' Tessa's eyes were warm. 'You know, Dr Llewellyn, I think I'm beginning to like you. Very, very much.'

'Good. I mean...great.' Mike clipped his words, desperately precluding further discussion. Domesticity was threatening to swamp him here. The feeling that this was right. That this was how it could be. That he was beginning to like this woman right back...

He walked over and scooped up a finger-load of fried onions, trying to shake off the feeling of unreality. Tess hauled the pan away with the firmness of a matriarch.

'No, you don't. Go and wash while I cook the steak. I'll bet you're all covered with patient or antiseptic or something disgusting and I won't have my steak compromised. Do you like it medium or rare? I don't do well done. It's a crime to burn meat like this.' She motioned to Mike's steaks—two enormous T-bones. 'We believe in steak in the US but I haven't seen steak like this for years.'

'Welcome to Australia, then, Dr Westcott.' Mike smiled faintly and went obediently towards the bathroom. As ordered. He walked slowly, though, and looked back over his shoulder at the slim girl presiding over his stove in her theatre gown and vivid curls. Good grief!

Mike did more than just wash. He changed from his tailored work trousers to casual jeans and open-necked shirt, taking the time to try and calm his thoughts. He emerged to his kitchenette to find Tess, minus her theatre gown now, attractively demure in her lovely white dress. She looked every inch the hostess as she served up two laden plates, with Mike her invited guest.

And Mike's pleasant, calm thoughts, which he'd taken such pains to achieve, got all stirred up again. He didn't speak. Even if he could have thought of something to say, he wasn't given the chance.

'Sit down,' his own personal matriarch ordered. 'I hope you don't mind me opening your wine. Hannah gave me the key to your apartment from the nurses' station. She looked at me every which way when I said we were eating together. Sort of with a ''you too'' look in her eye. And she wasn't very nice. Have you two had a relationship?'

Mike's eyebrows hit his hairline.

'No! I mean, I don't see what business it is—'

'So there's never been anything between you? Don't let your steak get cold,' Tess added kindly, as Mike sank down at the table. 'It's fabulous.'

'No.' Mike chopped into his steak and took a large mouthful of meat. His eyebrows rose even further. The wine marinade Tess had used on the steak was magnificent. 'Tessa, this is great.'

'It is, isn't it?' she said warmly. 'We *do* steak in the States, but you Aussies do *steak*!'

'Not like this we don't,' Mike said warmly. The sensation of coming home to this was almost taking his breath away.

'So tell me why Hannah Hester looked at me like she'd enjoy taking me out at dawn with a pistol apiece—with hers loaded and mine jinxed so it'd blow up in my hand.'

'I have no idea.'

'You haven't gone out with her?'

'Tessa, I don't know what business of yours my relationships are. What have you put on this steak? It's marvellous.'

'Red wine, garlic, lemon juice and a few herbs. Nothing special.' Tessa's face was serious as she spoke and he could see her mind wasn't on the meat. 'Mike, Hannah says I should make arrangements for Grandpa to move into the nursing home. She says its impossible for him to stay on the farm and she says I'll go around the twist here in a matter of months. She thinks I won't stay.'

'Yeah?' Mike sliced another piece of steak and it followed its predecessor. His smile faded to match Tessa's look of seriousness. Hannah Hester was an interfering busybody whose chief skill was upsetting relatives. If it wasn't so hard to find good nurses he'd sack her on the spot. And she'd upset Tessa...

The silence continued, but it wasn't uncomfortable. He watched Tessa's face as they ate, and finally he probed. 'Hannah's really upset you?'

'Worse than that,' Tess said. She finished the last of her steak and pushed her plate away. 'She upset Grandpa by talking right in front of him. She treated him as if he wasn't there, and any nurse worth her salt knows better than to think stroke victims can't hear. No matter how paralysed they are.'

He frowned. 'Tess, Hannah's a fine nurse.'

'She might be fine with her clinical skills, but she's not good with people. In fact, she's awful.'

Mike sighed. He could only agree. 'Tess, this place, well, it's a closed community. I know Hannah's not great. It's as if she has a permanent chip on her shoulder and, try as I may, I can never seem to get her on-side. I'll speak to her, but I can't afford to sack her and she knows it. Well-trained nurses are like hen's teeth around here. They're so scarce they hardly exist.'

'I know that,' Tess said tightly. 'That's the reason—the *only* reason—I didn't slug her.' She cheered up then, and smiled. Heavens, the girl was a real chameleon, changing in front of his eyes. 'That and the fact that she's bigger than me.'

'I see.' He grinned. 'I can just see the pair of you, slugging it out in the hospital corridor. Very professional.' His smile faded again. 'Seriously, Tess, you need to get along with the only professional staff the valley has. You value their skills, and in time you learn to undo the damage an uncaring person can do.'

'Yeah.' Her smile was back again now in force. 'I know. And I think I did. I told Grandpa he had to get better now, just to prove Hannah wrong. It's given him another motivation—as if he didn't have enough already.'

'See? You're learning.'

'Yeah, well, as long as she's just not being hurtful to Grandpa to get at me. Because she's jealous.'

'Well, that's just plain ridiculous,' he said firmly attacking his steak again.

'Why is it?' she asked slowly. 'Why is it ridiculous for Hannah to be jealous?'

'She has a boyfriend.'

'Did she have one when you first came back here?'

'No, but—'

'Then maybe she fell for you.'

'Women don't fall for me.'

Tess raised her eyebrows and said nothing. She finished her steak, carried her plate and wineglass to the sink, set her plate down and then stood and eyed Mike thoughtfully as he finished.

He could sense there was something coming here. Something really important. She had that 'major impertinence' look in her eye he was beginning to know. This woman didn't understand the meaning of the word personal.

And finally she said it.

'You're sure you're not gay, Dr Llewellyn?' She frowned into her wineglass and then fixed him with a speculative look. 'I know. You've told me you're not gay, but you're kind and you're sensitive and you're good-looking. You make good money and you drive a smashing car. So how that combination hasn't been grabbed and held onto...' She brought her eyebrows together and her eyes probed his—as though sticking an insect on a pin for examination. 'Are you *sure*?'

He might have known. He grinned. 'No, Dr Westcott, I am not gay,' he said firmly. He rose and carried his plate towards her.

Instinctively Tess took a step back, putting distance between herself and Mike until she had the information she wanted.

'Are you married, then? Divorced? Widowed? Separated?'

'Who wants to know?'

'Me,' she shot back at him.

'And what business is it of yours?'

'None at all,' she said calmly. 'But you're intending to be a working partner of mine and at least one nurse has now insinuated I'm setting my cap at you. I just want to know whether to tell her such a thing is ridiculous. And I'd really like to know that it's not.'

That was pretty blatant.

He blinked. What was happening here? Mike stared down at Tess and she stared straight back up at him—and he could read her mind like a book. It was almost as if she was propositioning him. If she'd been a man, she'd be buying roses and chocolates and laying siege....

Grabbing!

Whoa...

'It is ridiculous,' he said curtly. He gave her a strained look and put his plate on the sink. How the hell was he expected to handle this?

Tessa looked just lovely. Her soft, white dress was low-cut and clinging. Her eyes were huge in her elfin face and the few freckles scattered across the bridge of her nose were immensely—incredibly—appealing. They needed to be kissed.

Whoa!

'No, Dr Westcott,' he managed weakly, 'I'm not married, engaged, widowed, involved or even gay. But neither do I intend to be.'

'Why ever not?'

'I'm married to my work,' he said shortly.

'I've just taken a heap of your work off you. Does that mean I'll be hauled up before the divorce courts as co-respondent?'

Her voice was gently teasing, but he hardly heard. He stood by the sink and stared at her, fighting for control.

'There's more than enough work to keep us both frantic,' he told her heavily.

'But I don't intend to be frantic.' She lifted her chin. 'My medicine's important to me, but it's not everything. I still intend to look after my grandfather. I still intend to have a life.'

'My life is my medicine.'

'I can see that.' She moistened her lips. She felt strange. As if someone else was inside her body and that someone was a woman she hardly knew. That someone was so strongly drawn to Mike that she had hardly any control at all.

'It seems such a waste,' she murmured.

'A waste?' He looked sardonically at her. 'Waste for who?'

'A waste for me.'

Silence. The words echoed round and round the room, astounding in their simplicity.

'What on earth do you mean by that?' he said at last—and then his face closed as if he regretted the question.

Tess also should have regretted her statement. His question was a question Tess shouldn't be able to answer. She should just mumble an apology—give a silly giggle and get the hell out of here before she made a real fool of herself.

Instead, she took a long, deep breath and met his eyes with a look of pure defiance.

The woman's role was to stay demure and shy, Mike thought wildly. That was how he could cope. But how could he cope with a woman who was coming on like Tessa was coming on? Like she found him wildly attractive and didn't care who knew it. Especially she didn't mind if Mike knew it. She wanted him to know exactly how she felt, and how she felt was written right across her face.

'I mean that you're the most attractive male I've ever met,' she said softly. 'I mean that you're gentle and kind and caring and I just have to look at you and my knees sort of wobble underneath me. I mean that Hannah got it right when she said that one of the reasons I want to stay here is that I'd like to get to know you better.'

'She said that?'

'She said that. And it's true. Oh, it's not the only reason,' she added hastily as his face closed. 'Of course, I'm staying for my grandfather.' She took a deep breath, fighting for words. 'But if you want a partner with knees that don't wobble, you'd better tell me now that you find red hair a real turn-off. Or that you're into stamp collecting instead of women.' She gave a twisted smile. 'And I don't believe I'm saying this.'

'I don't believe you are either,' Mike said faintly. 'Women don't say these sort of things.'

'I just did.'

'Well, no one has before,' he said bluntly. 'Tess...'

'Don't tell me women don't find you attractive,' she shot at him. She took a deep breath and managed a smile. Damn, there was a glimmer behind her eyes that told Mike that a part of Tess was enjoying herself here. She was enjoying knocking his socks off.

And the rest!

Tess put her hands on the kitchen bench behind her and hitched herself up so she was sitting, her lovely stockinged legs swinging free as she watched the man before her. And he stared back at her as if she'd just crawled out of a spaceship!

'Maybe women have,' he admitted finally. 'But no one's told me.'

'Aw, gee… Poor little you. Hasn't anyone told you they find you very sexy?'

And Mike couldn't help himself. He burst out laughing.

'Tessa Westcott, you are incorrigible. I thought lady doctors—especially lady doctors trained in emergency medicine and who've seen everything the seamier side of life can throw at them—are supposed to be as sensible and hard-headed and as romantic as a brick.'

'They are,' she told him, and she grinned right back. She was crazy, but there was a very strong part of her that was enjoying being crazy. She'd just burned her bridges back to the States. In fact, she'd just abandoned a very sensible career plan and a very sensible boyfriend, albeit a very lukewarm one. If she wasn't a little crazy tonight, then she never would be.

'They say the only thing a sensible, committed female doctor with career ambition should love is a goldfish,' she said blithely. 'But I've thought it through, and I think you're much better than a goldfish.'

'Gee, thanks.' Mike looked at her for a long moment, and then walked two steps forward and took her hands in his. He had to make her see. 'Tess, this is crazy.'

It wasn't crazy at all. Taking her hands was a mistake. A huge mistake! The craziness disappeared right then and there as their hands touched.

'Crazy or not, it's the way I feel,' she said. Heaven knew how she kept her voice light, but somehow Tess managed it.

'Well, stop feeling like it.' He released her, but he didn't move. They were only inches apart, but Tessa's eyes were just above his from her perch on the bench. Hell, how to make her see that this link—what she said she could feel and what he could definitely feel—was totally, absolutely out of the question.

'Tessa, what I'm saying about work is true,' he managed. 'That's all I want. I have room for nothing else.'

'I'm very small,' Tess murmured. 'Couldn't you squash me in around the edges?'

'No.' He stopped smiling completely and took a step back. His face said the joke had gone far enough.

'You're not a priest,' Tess said gently. 'I'd love to know why you have room in your life for nothing but medicine.'

'I've seen what can happen when people forget their responsibilities.'

'I'm not asking you to forget your responsibilities.' Tess, too, had stopped smiling now. She jumped down from her bench and stepped forward—stepped forward so she was almost touching him. Her face said she had gone this far so she might as well try the whole bit.

'Mike, I'm not asking you to marry me,' she said, and somehow she forced her voice to stay light. 'What I'm saying is that there's something between us. Something…' She shrugged. 'I don't know what. It's a feeling I can't define. It's a feeling I've never felt in my life before and I want, more than anything, to explore it. That sounds wanton, doesn't it? As if I'm a loose woman. I'm not, Mike. I'm just… I just feel…'

And then her voice firmed, as if she was suddenly sure of her ground.

'I feel as if you're a part of me. That's crazy, isn't it?

But that's the way it is. So, tell me, Mike,' she demanded. 'Tell me that I'm a fool. Tell me that you feel nothing.'

'I don't want—'

'I'm not asking what you want. I'm asking what you feel.'

And then, before he could answer, she took one more step forward, put her arms up around his neck, stood on tiptoe—and she kissed him for all she was worth. And it was done so suddenly that there was nothing he could do to stop it.

It was *some* kiss.

It was a kiss of pure bravado, but it was more than that. It was a kiss that was full of questions, and it was a kiss full of wonder.

Tess had never done such a thing in her life before. Her act might have seemed wanton—forward—but there was nothing of that in her kiss. Her lips were gentle, sweet and unsure, as if she really wanted to touch him. It was as if her body was drawn to him like a bee to honey, and she was half expecting to be drawn so far into the sweetness that she'd drown.

And he...

The last thing he wanted to do was to kiss this woman. He didn't. And yet her lips were touching his and her body was soft and yielding and...and so lovely!

When her mouth touched his, the kiss slammed home the knowledge that this was something outside his ken. She was so desirable...

Sure, he'd kissed other women. Hell, he'd made a vow, but that vow hadn't been one of chastity. His vow had been one of emotional detachment. He'd made love to women before, but they'd always known the rules. No involvement. There had never been any promises of tomorrow. There was only passion on his terms.

But this...this wasn't on his terms. This was on no one's

terms because, as their lips met, it was like two pieces of a shattered whole being joined. More, it was like tinder to fuel. Apart they were nothing—cold and useless. Together they were fire.

Mike's body stilled in shock, but Tessa's arms came around him again, soft and yet urgent, pulling him against her, and suddenly nothing in his life had ever felt so right, so complete. There were forces working here that were beyond his control, he thought wildly. This was beyond anything he'd ever known before. The desire to respond to this lovely thing…this woman who was so unknown…was almost overwhelming.

Her lips were soft and warm and urgent. She smelt of flowers, of sunshine and of warmth, and he could no more resist her loveliness than he could stop himself breathing.

He wasn't breathing. He wasn't sure what he was doing.

He couldn't help himself. He *must* respond. His hands fell to hold Tessa against him, glorying in the way her breasts pressed against his chest. His mouth responded to her kiss, tasting her…wanting her.

And wanting more…

Dear God, what could he do with this? He'd never known he could feel this way. His vow had been made without knowing this wonder, and if he'd known… If he'd known he had this need—that somewhere in the world was a woman like this—could he have made his vow? But he'd made the vow, and the vow still stood.

Somehow he managed to pull back. Somehow he managed to put her away from him and hold her at arm's length, and he stared down at her with eyes that were confused and desperate.

'Tess, no…'

'Well, now I know,' Tess managed, in a voice that was barely above a whisper and held an obvious tremor.

'Know what?'

'You're certainly not gay.' She tried to smile but it didn't quite come off. 'Wow!'

'Wow' was right. And where to go from here?

The phone. Glory be, the phone. Its shrill ring sounded from the living room and Mike headed there like a drowning man headed for a life-raft.

'Hello?'

'Dr Llewellyn?' It was Mavis, at Reception. 'Is that you?' It obviously didn't sound like him.

'Yes.' Mike cleared his throat, and with a superhuman effort managed not to look back to where Tess was standing, watching from the doorway. 'Of course. Mavis, what is it?'

'I've just had a call from Kylie Wisen,' Mavis told him and her voice was apologetic. It was as though she knew she was interrupting something, and she'd just love to know what. 'You know Kylie?'

Mike's head clicked into medical mode with a visible effort and he gave his mental case file a quick search. 'Kylie. That's Bill and Claire Wisen's kid. Seventeen years old. Peroxided hair and half a dozen earrings.'

'That's the one.' Mavis sighed. 'She's looking after her sister's two-year-old while her sister and her husband go out to dinner and then go on to the shire ball. But…'

'But?'

'But the little one—Sally McPherson—has stuck her big toe in the bath outlet.' Mavis sighed again. 'I'm really sorry, Doctor, but they've tried everything to get it out and I think you'll have to go.'

Go? Of course he had to go. Thanks be…

'I'll be there in five minutes,' Mike said strongly, still not looking at Tess. 'Mavis, ring Kylie back and tell her I'm coming. Tell her the most important thing is not to let Sally pull. If the toe gets swollen from tugging then we'll be in all sorts of trouble.'

He replaced the receiver and finally turned to face Tess again.

'I need to go,' he said.

'I know.' Her eyes didn't leave his face. 'I heard. Can I come?'

'Tess...'

'The sooner I get to know the people of this town, the better it'll be for both of us.' She glanced at her watch. 'I have an hour before I promised Louise I'd mom-sit, and you have an hour before you need to go your ball. Strop's not much company—so let's go unstick toes.'

'I—'

'Don't you want me?' She let her face fall, like a child deprived of a lolly.

Hell, he couldn't work with her, he thought desperately, watching her face and trying to figure out whether to laugh or to groan. He couldn't!

But he sure as hell couldn't tell her he didn't want her.

'Fine, then,' he said in a voice that indicated he'd been goaded beyond belief. 'Fine. Let's go do some medicine. It might get your mind off sex.'

'Hey, my mind's not on sex,' she teased gently, her eyes laughing up at him. And then the smile died a little. 'My mind doesn't get past your face.' Then she gave an honest little shrug and her smile came back in full. 'Well...for the moment.'

Sally was still attached to her bath. They arrived to find neighbours, two members of the fire brigade, a mechanic and a hefty plumber complete with dangerous-looking tool set, all trying to wedge into one small farmhouse bathroom. Mike had obviously been the last of a long line of people appealed to.

Sally McPherson was two years old and in deep distress. She was huddled naked and sobbing in the empty bath, and her sobs were those of a child who'd gone past expecting help. The noise in the little room was overwhelming.

'Let's clear this room,' Tess suggested firmly, as Mike went straight to the little girl. He saw her need. The child was sitting alone in the empty bathtub, and why the hell wasn't anyone in there holding her?

'Right.' Mike reached in and held the little girl's shoulders, gripping her tight. 'OK, Sally. We'll get you out of here soon, but first let's get you warm.'

'We need Sally's parents and the plumber,' Tessa said brusquely, and Mike gave her a wondering glance. She'd snapped straight back into medical mode. What had taken place between them belonged somewhere else. She was now crisp, decisive and every inch a doctor trained to cope with trauma. 'The rest of you, I'd like you to stay outside until you're needed. Now, who's Sally's mom?'

'She's not here,' a girl with peroxided blonde hair and too much make-up told her. 'I'm Kylie, the kid's aunty. My sister and her husband have gone out to dinner and I don't know where they've gone. It was supposed to be the pub but it's burned down so they went somewhere else.' She glared aggressively, as though expecting Tess to turn on her and say it was all her fault.

'One of the neighbours is doing a ring-round of their friends to try and find them,' the plumber volunteered. He turned to Mike who was lifting the child forward to take the strain from the toe.

'Doc, I've been thinking,' he said. 'The hassle with the outlet on old baths is that the outlets don't screw. Usually it's a cinch if a kid gets stuck because you just turn the whole outlet around while someone turns the kid at the same time—so they both come out together and at least you can work on getting the thing off when they're out of the bath. This is an old type, though. It's a permanent fixture—glued fast.'

'Then we'll have to chip it out,' Mike said. He was practically in the bath now, gathering the child to him. 'She's freezing. I want blankets and hot-water bottles. Fast.'

'I figured you'd say chip it,' the plumber said in satisfaction. 'I've got the tools here ready. I would have done it before but I didn't like to when the kiddy was so distressed and thrashing about, like. I reckon, though, what's best'd be if I get underneath the house and cut through the pipe. Then if I chip it from underneath I won't upset the kid as much. With luck the whole thing will lift up. It'll just be a matter of supporting the kid while we do it.'

'Do it,' Mike said, his eyes on the little girl's face. They needed to get her out of there fast. She was showing signs of going into shock.

'Could you hop in the bath and cuddle her?' Tess asked Kylie. She cast a quick glance at Mike, and Mike nodded his agreement. Warmth and reassurance were what this child needed more than anything.

'What…hop in?' The teenage babysitter was clearly horrified.

'Do as she says, Kylie,' Mike ordered, and Tess almost grinned as the teenager gazed at Mike in dismay but then did what she was told. Mike had some authority in this town. There weren't many people who could tell a teenager to sit in a bath in front of witnesses and be obeyed.

In two minutes they had the sulky teenager sitting right in the bath, with the child lying back on her lap. Without her mum to comfort the child, it was the best they could hope for. While Mike examined the toe, Tess sent a couple of the women to find hot-water bottles, and she replaced the single towel around the child's body with a big fluffy blanket.

'She's been pulling,' Mike said softly, looking from the swollen toe to the white, drained face of the little girl. The fact that the child was now silent was ominous. The old medical adage was, 'Never worry too much about a child who's screaming. If a child's quiet, then worry.'

'I think we might administer some pethidine, Dr Westcott,' Mike said, and Tess nodded. She retrieved what he needed from his bag and prepared it.

'There's no way we'll get the toe out by pulling.' Mike's fingers were carefully probing the little foot. 'The whole foot's swollen now. Our best chance is to manoeuvre it free once we have both sides exposed.'

There was a thumping under the house and the sound of men's voices. The plumber obviously had back-up. The child started whimpering again, and Kylie put her face in the child's hair.

'Hey, hush, Sally, Sally,' Kylie said softly. 'We've got two doctors on top and a big plumber underneath, cutting your toe out. We'll be able to take the pipe to playschool for show and tell, and if we're lucky the fireman might give you a ride in the fire engine.'

'Good girl,' Tess said warmly. Underneath the make-up and the earrings and the bravado, there was a good kid. Kylie must have been almost as scared as Sally, facing this on her own.

The change in Kylie seemed to affect Sally—or maybe it was the pethidine kicking in. The little girl lay slumped on Kylie's lap and let them do as they willed, and five minutes later the whole bath outlet and three inches of outlet pipe lifted upwards and the little foot was free.

Free from the bath, but not from the pipe.

'Now what?' Kylie said uneasily, gathering the little girl closer, pipe and all.

'We get her to the hospital,' Mike said. He could see the tip of the toe now and he wasn't happy. It had no colour at all. There wasn't time to immobilise it and wait for the swelling to settle before they tried to free it.

'I want my mummy,' the child whimpered and buried her head in Kylie's breast.

'Yeah, well, I ought to have found out where they were going,' Kylie muttered, close to tears herself, and Mike put his hand on her shoulder.

'They should have told you. Let's not blame yourself here, Kylie. You're doing a great job.' Then he looked at Tess, his mind working over options. 'How do you feel about giving an anaesthetic, Dr Westcott? Under supervision, of course.'

Tess met his look, and bit her lip.

She knew what he was asking here. Mike Llewellyn was asking an unregistered doctor to give a general anaesthetic to a child without her parents' consent.

If she didn't, the child would lose her big toe. And if she did...the legal ramifications were vast.

'Tess, there's no choice,' Mike said heavily. 'I know it's a lot to ask but I'll take all legal responsibility. I'll put it in writing if you like.'

'You trust me?'

'Yes,' he said, and he did. He met her look and he nodded. Yes, he was sure. Tess might be flirtatious and frivolous, but he had the gut feeling that, whatever else she was, she was a damned fine doctor.

'OK, let's do it,' Tess said softly. She smiled at Kylie, a big, cheery smile that was meant to totally reassure her. 'Isn't it lucky that I came all the way from the States?' she said. 'I must have just known that Dr Llewellyn couldn't manage even a stuck toe without me.'

Much to Mike's relief, they got the toe out without sawing the bath pipe right back to the skin.

Tessa's anaesthetic procedure was extremely competent, as Mike had guessed it would be, and once he'd reassured himself that she knew exactly what she was doing he was free to deal with the toe.

Their friendly plumber, looking like a big green bear with his overalls covered by a theatre gown, cut the pipe again, this time half an inch from the toe. That meant Mike could work on the toe from both sides.

He applied cold compresses to the toe. The nurse—the horrible Hannah who was *so* nice in Mike's presence—applied warm cloths to the metal to get maximum expansion, while Mike carefully applied lubricant to the toe. Then, with gentle pressure from the front of the toe, he was able to finally push from one side and pull from the other.

The toe came free with a pop, and Tess looked up from her dials to see colour seeping back into it almost instantaneously.

'Oh, well done,' she said, and she started reversal straight away. There was no point keeping Sally asleep a moment longer than needed, and there was now no drama.

'Well done to you, Tess,' Mike said softly, looking along the table to where she was carefully monitoring Sally's breathing. He hadn't been in the least concerned about the anaesthetic, he realised as he gently massaged the little toe. One look at Tessa's confident preparation had put his mind at ease. The lady knew her job.

So now what? he thought. Now what?

It was almost unbelievable. Out of the blue he'd been granted one fine doctor—a doctor with skills in anaesthetics and trauma medicine. If he'd hunted Australia for a new partner, he couldn't have found anyone better.

Once she was registered there was nothing they couldn't do, he thought suddenly—jubilantly. All the minor surgery that he currently sent away...the road accidents that he couldn't cope with on his own...the urgent stuff. He'd lost patients in the past because there'd been only one of him when he'd needed two.

If she really was willing to stay...

She was, he knew she was, but there were strings. Or rather, there was a string. One string—and that string was emotional involvement. Hell, he could have this girl as a partner and keep his distance. He must! He couldn't think clearly when she was near. His mind felt weird now—fuzzed at the edges. It was the way he'd always known he'd feel if ever he let go.

'There's no need for you to stay now,' he told Tess brusquely, and even Hannah threw him a curious glance. He sounded strained and angry—not as if he'd just performed a successful operation. 'If you're supposed to be looking after Louise's mum...'

'Mmm.' Tess glanced at her watch and then back to Mike, her face expressionless. 'The ball starts at nine. That's twenty minutes ago. Aren't you due to be there?'

'I'm meeting Liz inside.'

'Liz?'

'My date.'

'Oh, right. Of course. Your date.' Tessa's eyes twinkled a little. 'Not your lover?'

'Tess...'

'OK, OK.' She held up her hands in mock defeat and looked down at the pathetic little bundle coming into life on the table. 'I'm off. You take care good of Sally.' There had been no need to say that—she knew he would. 'I'll tell Kylie that she can come in now, shall I? And her parents? Are they here yet?'

'If they're not, I'll stay here until they come,' he said heavily. 'And until Sally's fully out of the anaesthetic. Liz won't mind if I'm late.'

'I'll bet she will,' Tess said softly, thoughtfully. 'I'll just bet she will mind, Mike Llewellyn, but she won't say so. It seems to me that you have the ladies in the valley too well trained for their own good.'

'I'd drink to that,' Hannah retorted before she could stop herself, and Tess grinned.

So did Hannah, which left Mike feeling…

Stupid?

CHAPTER EIGHT

AS BALLS went, it was a fizzer.

Maybe it was the tragedy of the fire the night before that was casting a pall over the night, or maybe it was just that Mike wasn't in the mood for dancing.

It wasn't his partner's fault. Liz was at her vivacious best, svelte and lovely in shimmering black and silver. Usually he enjoyed her company. Liz was a hard-headed career woman with no aspirations for emotional entanglements, and with her he could dance, knowing there was no hidden agenda.

Or could he?

Tessa's words still stung.

'Liz, do you think I'm a bastard?' he asked, as the evening drew to a close. The music was slowing and couples were dancing cheek to cheek.

Liz was dancing easily in his arms, matching his steps superbly, but there was no desire on either part for them to dance any closer.

'What do you mean?'

'I've had it implied that I'm a heartless bastard for not taking out any girl more than twice.'

'You've taken me out more than twice.'

'That's different.'

Liz grinned. 'Yeah. But that's because I'm also a heartless bastard. ''Love 'em and leave 'em''—that's my motto. My dad was like that, and I am, too. There's no way any man's going to tie me down. You and I suit very well, Dr Llewellyn.' Her grin deepened. 'But don't get any ideas about us suiting too well or I'll run a mile.'

He smiled back. Right. It was fine.

It was fine with Liz, but what about the other women? Women like Hannah, whom he'd dated twice and when she'd clung he'd put away fast. Maybe Tess was right. It wasn't fair.

So where did that leave him, then? Should he only be dating women like Liz?

Yes. A vow was a vow!

Just on midnight he got another call. Mavis rang from the hospital to say Myrtle Jefferson had suffered a fall and needed an urgent house call. It seemed Myrtle had taken an hour to crawl to the phone to call for help, but when Mavis had offered to send the ambulance the old lady had become almost hysterical. She'd told Mavis she only needed the doctor. She needed Mike, she'd wept, but she needed no one else.

It was almost a relief to leave. He left Liz to the attentions of the remaining Bellanor bachelors, and Liz didn't mind him going in the least.

So... That was the way he wanted it—wasn't it?

Yes, it had to be, so concentrate on medicine, he told himself fiercely. Concentrate on Myrtle. His medicine had to be the only thing that mattered.

Myrtle certainly needed him. It took him ten minutes to get into the house because she wasn't capable of reaching the front door to unlock it. In the end he broke a bathroom window, to find her lying on the hall floor by the phone. She'd broken her hip, but what was of even more concern to the old lady was that she'd lost control of her bladder.

Myrtle was rigid with mortification, and it took him a while to figure out just how much of her distress could be put down to embarrassment and how much was due to pain.

'It's OK, Myrtle,' he told her. 'No one's going to judge

you by this. It often happens after an accident—even to young, fit teenagers.'

But Myrtle would have none of it. She sobbed weakly in distress so, despite his reluctance to move her more than necessary, he administered morphine and then set himself to fix things. By the time the ambulance arrived, Myrtle had been sponged with warm water and was dressed in a clean, soft nightgown. Her soiled night things were soaking in the laundry.

'Now no one will ever know except you and me,' he told her, smiling. 'And you and I go back a long way, Myrtle. I reckon you might even have changed a nappy or two of mine, so that must make us about quits.'

'I reckon that's right,' she said weakly, clutching his hand in gratitude. 'You were the sweetest little boy. And you've turned out... Well, your mother would be proud of you. This new lady doctor's a lucky young woman.'

'This new lady doctor...?'

'Mrs Abbot saw her at surgery this morning and she told Henrietta Smiggins and Henrietta told me. She's just what you need.' The morphine was kicking in, her dignity was restored and Myrtle was bouncing back to her old impertinent self.

'As a medical partner—'

'No, dear.' Myrtle patted his arm and fixed him with a knowing look. 'As a proper partner. That's what you need, dear. You need a wife, and I won't let you tell me any different.'

'Myrtle—'

'I think I need to go to sleep now, dear,' Myrtle said weakly, closing her eyes on his protest. 'I just thought you ought to know...the whole valley's very happy for you. And so am I. You and Henry's granddaughter... Well, well.'

He couldn't stand it.

Tessa had been in the town for a whole three days and the entire district was matchmaking. He travelled back to the hospital behind the ambulance with his mouth set in a grim, angry line.

This was nonsense, stupid, crazy stuff. Fluff! It seemed like the whole town was going nuts.

'Everyone except me is crazy here,' he said into the night. 'I'm not going nuts. I'm the one that's level-headed here. For heaven's sake, if she thinks she can bulldoze me…' His voice died away.

If Tess thought she could bulldoze him, how on earth was he to stop himself being bulldozed?

It took a while to settle Myrtle. He X-rayed her hip and, at Myrtle's insistence, decided on a conservative approach. The bone wasn't displaced. With care and bed rest she could recover without internal splinting. Splinting required a trip to an orthopaedic surgeon in Melbourne and a general anaesthetic, and Myrtle wasn't having a bar of it.

'Myrtle, it'll mean up to ten weeks of bed rest if we don't send you to Melbourne,' he told her. 'It'll take you much longer to recover.'

'I don't care.'

'If you get it splinted you could be up and about much sooner.'

'I'm not leaving here.'

'If you stay, you risk pneumonia,' he told her gently. 'There's also the problem of pressure sores and increased difficulty of getting you mobile again afterwards. Myrtle, at your age—'

'I don't care what I risk,' she told him. 'I'll lie here and wiggle my toes and keep my circulation going so I won't have a problem. And at my age I'm well old enough to decide for myself. I'm staying here.'

Maybe she was right. Myrtle was nearly ninety so there

were risks whatever course of action Mike decided on. With immobilisation she risked complications, but by giving her a general anaesthetic and putting her through the trauma of travelling to the city maybe she risked worse.

And she was absolutely definite. 'I've lived my whole life here and this is where I'll die,' she told him. 'So if there's a chance this'll kill me, I'd rather take the chance that it'll kill me here.'

'I doubt it'll kill you,' he told her, adjusting the lines on gentle traction. 'You're tough as old boots.'

'Well, even old boots crack in the end,' she said wearily. 'And now... I pulled you away from the ball. You go back and enjoy yourself.'

She was wonderful. Mike looked down at her with affection, and suddenly thought this was how Tess would end up. A feisty old lady, loving to the end.

Tess...

He didn't do as Myrtle had ordered. He didn't return to the ball. The ball would be over by now and Liz wouldn't have waited for him. She knew better than that. He wouldn't mind betting she'd have latched onto another eligible bachelor for a ride home, and he didn't mind at all.

Now if it had been Tess...

It hadn't been Tess. Stop thinking like that!

He paused in the corridor, strangely unsettled. It was one a.m. It was time he was in bed, but he didn't feel in the least tired. Strop would still be snoring. After such an exciting event as a football match he'd likely sleep for a week, so there was nothing calling him home.

He'd just check on Sally, he decided. They were keeping the little girl in overnight to make sure the anaesthetic wore off with no ill effects. Her mother and father had been in earlier, abandoning their intention to go on to the ball, but he imagined they'd have gone home now.

So he'd just check...

He opened the door of the children's ward, and Tess was there. She was sitting in a chair beside the cot, and she had Sally cuddled in her arms. In the half-dark, with her back to him, Tess was totally oblivious to anything but the toddler in her arms. She was humming the little one to sleep.

He stopped short.

For a long moment he stared. Tess didn't see him. Her face was in the baby's hair and she was crooning silly, half-remembered lullabies. She rocked and sang, and Sally whimpered and snuggled in half-sleep.

Dear God, she was beautiful.

Mike couldn't turn his head away. He couldn't back out. He stood like he'd been struck.

Tess still didn't see him. She was wholly concerned with what she was doing, and she had no thoughts for anything but the little one in her arms.

He swallowed and closed his eyes. Hell! Tess had spent the first part of tonight babysitting Louise's mum so Louise could have a chance at a love life, and then she'd made the effort to come back into the hospital to check on a toddler she cared about.

She had a heart so big…so warm…

Somehow he managed to get himself out into the corridor, but he didn't know how.

This, then, was what he'd vowed never to have, he thought bitterly. He'd never understood the consequences of his vow so clearly until now. Up to this moment, his vow had been easy to keep. There'd been no one like this to tempt him.

The thought of his mother swept across his mind. Dead… When a decent doctor—a doctor who'd had his mind on his job—could have saved her life.

This woman—Tessa—did have the power to distract him, he knew. She had the power to make him think of something other than medicine, and he dared not risk it.

There was no way he was getting personally involved with this woman!

His mother deserved better than this. His mother deserved that he keep his vow. He kept the vision of his mother in his head, and he held it as if he'd drown if he let it go. No! He couldn't let himself be swayed.

Damn her. She'd have to go.

But he couldn't make her go. The valley needed Tess almost as much as it needed him.

Swearing softly to himself, he made his way back along the darkened corridor. A nurse came out of Henry Westcott's room—it was the horrible Hannah—and she lifted surprised eyebrows at the sight of Mike.

'I thought you'd gone to bed. Myrtle's resting peacefully. There's no need—'

'Is Henry awake?'

'He is,' Hannah told him, obviously even more surprised by his curtness. 'I've just given him a rub. He's been complaining that the pressure sores are hurting.'

Mike frowned. He really didn't like Hannah on night duty. She meant well, and she would have given Henry an efficient and effective rub, but her words were often capable of inflicting more hurt than her hands could heal. And at night and alone in a hospital bed, everything seemed so much more bleak.

'I'll go in and see him.'

'Suit yourself.' Hannah shrugged and moved off down the corridor toward the lights of the nurses' station. 'If you don't think you're better off sleeping…'

Her inference was obvious. Talking to old men in the middle of the night just for the sake of talking, that was a waste of time. Hannah would never do it. She'd do what had to be done medically and no more.

She wasn't like Tess, Mike thought bleakly. Tess, sitting up half the night to keep a grumpy old lady happy and free her daughter to enjoy herself, and then returning to the hospital to give a two-year-old a cuddle…

No wonder he'd never been tempted to break his vow when he dated the likes of Hannah, he thought. There was no comparison at all.

'Goodnight, Hannah,' he said firmly, and he pushed open Henry's door. He'd check on Henry no matter how much a waste of time Hannah thought it. Maybe he needed a top-up of painkillers.

Henry was wide awake. The old man was watching the opening door with hopeful eyes and Mike smiled in sympathy as he saw the old man's face fall. That the old man was hoping the visitor would be Tessa was painfully obvious.

'Tessa's in the children's ward,' Mike said softly. 'Do you want me to fetch her?'

'No…' Henry gave a wheezy cough. He fought to get his breath as the door swung closed. 'No. I don't need her. I don't need anyone. You should all be asleep, not wasting time on me.'

Mike looked at him more closely, hearing the rough emotion in the tired old voice. 'What's wrong, Henry? Pain?'

'No. The rub helped.'

'Has Hannah been upsetting you?'

'No. No…'

'She has. I can hear it in your voice.' Mike walked across to the bed and dragged up a chair. 'Hannah's technically one of my best nurses,' he told Henry gently. 'She never puts a foot wrong, but as for her mouth… Medically she might never put her foot wrong, but when her foot's not in use she stores it in her mouth. Tell me what she's been saying.'

'Just…'

'Just?'

'She's just been telling me how good the nursing home here is.'

'Yeah?'

'It's not a bad place to end up, I suppose,' Henry said wearily. 'Good as anywhere.'

'As good as your farm?'

'No, but—'

'But nothing,' Mike said solidly. Damn Hannah. He'd have to give her a few solid orders about what she could and couldn't talk to patients about. 'Tessa has you all sorted out,' he told the old man. 'Like it or not, she's dragging you back out to your farm as soon as you're on your feet, and she has every intention of you and her and Doris the pig living happily ever after.'

'That's no life for a girl.'

'Says who?'

'Says Hannah. It'd be all right if she was right...'

'If who was right?'

'Tessa. Tess says...' Henry paused for a moment to cough. He was still as weak as be damned. It took him two minutes before he collected himself enough to continue, but Mike waited as if he had all the time in the world. This was important.

And finally it came. 'Tess says it's not just she and me and Doris,' Henry managed. 'It's...'

'It's?'

Henry hesitated, and then his face creased into a shamefaced grin. 'It's you, boy,' he confessed. 'Tess told me she intends to marry you.' Then, as Mike's face stilled, he hurried into an explanation.

'Oh, she was just kidding, mind. I told her I wouldn't have her wasting her life here and she said, nonsense, her intended husband lived here and she had no intention of leaving. Ever. So I thought...' He smiled. 'Maybe it's nonsense but I thought...just for a bit, until I felt more myself…I'd let myself believe it. Only…I told Hannah, just as a joke, like. And Hannah says that's crazy because there's no way you'll ever marry anyone, even someone like Hannah or Liz Hayes, much less Tessa.'

Good grief. What was he to say to this?

'But, Henry, I've only known your granddaughter for three days,' Mike said helplessly. He was totally at sea here. It was as if he were being washed by waves he couldn't even see. 'That's crazy.'

'Yeah.' Henry grimaced. 'But Tess said three minutes was enough for her. She knew.' He sighed heavily and tried to twist in bed. His paralysed side held him back. He gave a grunt of frustration and Mike moved to ease him over.

'Her grandma was the same,' Henry said finally when he was comfortable again. 'Tessa's grandma took one look at me and told me that was *it*. Forget bachelorhood, she told me. I was the one. It took Ellen a year to talk me round, but I might have saved myself the effort of fighting. Marrying Ellen was the best thing I ever did. But you…'

'But I'll not be talked around,' Mike said heavily. 'This is nonsense.' He took a deep breath. 'So is the thought of a nursing home for you. There's a job and a life for your granddaughter in this valley without me in the equation. So let's just make you comfortable and get you back onto your feet and back to Doris. Doris…now, there's a nice, uncomplicated female.'

'Ain't no such thing,' Henry said morosely. 'Uncomplicated female? Hah!'

Mike spent most of what little remained of the night staring sleeplessly at the ceiling. About dawn he fell into an uneasy slumber but at seven Strop heaved himself up on the bed and took over the pillow—and by eight Mike was up and ready for work.

In work lay his salvation.

Sunday morning was his easiest time, and it was often his only rest for the week. There was no surgery. He ran an evening clinic for urgent cases—mostly just to lighten his load on Mondays—but apart from emergencies he was free.

There was nothing urgent happening in the hospital this morning, and after Tessa's intervention there was nothing hanging over from the day before.

He let Sally go home with her relieved parents—proudly carrying her 'toe ring'. He talked Jason through accepting a full tear of his Achilles tendon and the possibility of fixing it in the valley if Tessa's registration came through. He made sure Myrtle was comfortable and settled and still determined to stay where she was, and then he turned his attention to the rest of the day.

Tess was nowhere to be seen. He'd visited Henry but Henry was visitor-free and sleeping soundly, no doubt tired after his busy social life the night before. Louise was acting charge nurse, cheerful and still slightly flushed after her night at the ball.

'Tess went out to the farm early,' she told him. 'She's moving there today.'

Great. That meant he had the hospital to himself.

The day suddenly seemed drab and totally uninteresting.

There was one really nasty task that had to be done. Sam Fisher's dental records had been dropped off at the surgery the night before. Mike mentally squared his shoulders and headed down to the morgue.

By the time he'd finished making absolutely certain that what lay there was definitely what remained of Sam, the day seemed more than just drab. He was depressed past belief.

Hell!

So, now what?

He collected Strop and emerged from the hospital to brilliant autumn sunshine. The day was gorgeous. He stood in the car park breathing in huge lungfuls of fresh air, trying to drive away the smell and remembrance of what he'd just done.

Who'd be a doctor?

It did have advantages. One of them lay just before him. His Aston Martin was the pride of his life. It was a bit dog-haired, but it was still gorgeous.

It needed a woman in the passenger seat, he decided, looking at it with affection. Not a dopey Basset. To really set it off, it needed a woman, with red hair flying free…

Oh, terrific. He was going nuts here. What the hell was he thinking of? He'd known Tess for three days and he was going nuts.

Strop cast him a reproachful look and he laughed and climbed into the driver's seat. 'OK, I'm not thinking of replacing you. Or maybe I could get you a cushion so the gearshift doesn't bruise your butt.'

More dirty looks, and Mike grinned. Strop knew the priorities. He needed no one else in this car. No one!

Maybe he should go and collect Liz. She'd always come for a drive with him. But…she didn't like Strop.

So… He'd go for a drive with just Strop.

He didn't. Instead, he nosed his beloved car northwards, up toward the mountains. He had his phone on his belt. He could be contacted if needed. He'd just see…

And the sleek sports car purred its way straight to Henry Westcott's farm, and it turned into Henry's gate as if it were magnetised. It was just to see that Tess didn't need help, he told himself firmly, but he didn't believe it for a minute.

It was just because he wanted to see Tess. Hell, he had the self-control of a mating newt!

Tess was in the shed with Doris. Today she was dressed for farm business, with stained jeans that were just a tad too tight—gloriously too tight—a work-stained T-shirt and a gorgeous blue scarf, tying back her red curls.

As Mike entered the shed, Strop at his heels, he found her squatting beside the piglets, deep in conversation with Doris.

'I don't know how you can tell them apart because I can't,' she was telling the sow. 'You need hospital wristbands. Trotter bands. Though this little one…he's fatter than the rest. Let's call this one Mike, shall we?'

'Why? Because I'm fatter than the rest?'

'Oh…' Tess swung around to face him, and her face flushed scarlet. 'Whoops. I didn't know.' She scrambled to her feet, and then she smiled and there was no disguising her pure, unmitigated pleasure that he'd come. Mike felt himself warm from the toes up at her welcome. 'I didn't dare hope you'd come,' she told him.

'So this is a private name-calling ceremony?'

'It's a family affair,' she agreed. 'Just me and Doris and the kids.'

'Are we intruding?'

'No, not at all,' she said cordially. 'Unless Strop is interested in piglet.'

'Only roasted. That old idea of catching and killing your own meal was bred out of Strop's remaining brain cell generations ago.'

Tess grinned as Strop wandered outside to see if roast pork was somewhere else. 'Then Doris and I are really pleased to see you,' she said.

The warmth grew warmer—and Mike struggled to keep his face straight.

'So…why are we calling the fat pig Mike?'

'Well…' Tess had her equilibrium back now. She picked up the proposed Mike piglet and surveyed him, nose to nose. Unbothered, Doris suckled on. Some sows took umbrage to having their family handled, but as far as Doris was concerned Tess, it seemed, could do anything she liked.

'Is it just because he's fat?' Mike enquired again, inspecting the piglet closely.

'Well, there is that,' Tess agreed. She grinned and checked Mike out. It was all Mike could do not to blush as her assessing gaze raked him from the toes up. 'But you're not really fat,' she added kindly. 'You're just...well, just sort of muscled.'

And then Tessa's grin deepened and she swung the little piglet around so his tail was in the air. 'But there's another resemblance. Look at this. He *does* look like you, Mike Llewellyn. He has the cutest butt!'

'Gee, thanks!' The girl was incorrigible. Hell, he *was* blushing.

She chuckled, unabashed, and gently laid Mike Piglet down on the straw with his brothers and sisters. Mike Piglet headed teat-ward, seemingly at the speed of light, and Tess chuckled again, before turning back to Mike Person.

'You know, you look really appealing when you're embarrassed,' she told him kindly. 'You're almost as cute as little Mike and his brothers and sisters—Oinks One to Seven.'

And then she really looked at him. Her smile died and her eyes became searching.

'Mike, what's wrong?'

'There's nothing—'

She took a step forward. 'Oh, God... Is it Grandpa?' The colour drained from Tessa's face and he spoke quickly to reassure her

'Henry's fine.'

'Then why do your eyes look like that?' And then Tessa's face cleared as she figured it out. 'Oh, Mike. I forgot. I know what it is. The dental records arrived last night. You've been identifying Sam.'

She could read him like a book! He took a step back, as though putting distance between himself and Tess, but Tess wasn't having it. She walked over and gave him a king-sized hug, and it was all he could do not to hug her back.

'I should have come with you,' she said softly. 'I could have helped. It must have been awful.'

'No.'

'Oh, no,' she jeered. 'Not awful. Don't forget, I saw him, Mike. It *was* awful. And you were his friend.'

'Tess…' He stopped, unable to go on. For the life of him he didn't know what to say, or how on earth to respond. Since his mother had died all those years ago, nothing and no one had been allowed close. To have this girl know intuitively what was wrong…and to hug him like this…and to care…

The sensation was insidious in its sweetness.

'It's OK. You can admit it was awful, but at least now it's done. And the end for Sam must have been fast.' She gave him another hug and stepped back so she could see him again while he was still figuring out how to respond. But he didn't need to respond.

'Come in and see what I've done to the house,' she begged, and she took his hand and dragged him out of the barn before he could protest. Her hand held his in a grip which warmed him from the fingers up and which wouldn't be denied. There was nothing for Mike to do but be propelled forward.

She didn't stop until she reached the kitchen, and he stopped, stunned, as he walked in the door. What she'd done here…

The place had been transformed.

It was clean for a start. The house in Henry Westcott's care had been left to deteriorate. Henry's wife had been house-proud, but after she'd died Henry had simply not cared. He'd kept it clean enough basically, but that had been all.

The last time Mike had been in here—the night they'd found Henry—the place had been dark and smoke-stained and dreary. But now…

'How long have you been here?' Mike asked faintly, staring around at the transformation.

'Since about seven. I couldn't sleep. Louise's mum snores and Louise was due on duty early, so we had breakfast together and talked about how wonderful Harvey Begg is. She even loves his Volvo.' Tessa's voice sounded awed. She smiled and kept on.

'I left her stargazing and hiked in to the hospital, said hi to Grandpa, who was snoring as loudly as Louise's mum, and then borrowed a pile of cleaning stuff from the store. I needed more but Mr Harcourt, the man who owns the hardware shop, was picking up his newspaper from his front lawn as I drove past. I know him from yesterday when I treated his cough. I was very kind about his smoking habits—apart from telling him he'd be dead in two years if he didn't cut down, I wasn't threatening or anything.'

Tess paused to catch her breath, and then she kept right on going.

'Anyway, Mr Harcourt was embarrassed about being caught in his pyjamas. They have yellow ducks all over them! They were a gift from his wife, he says, though I don't know whether I believe him. I think he likes them. And he was smoking again this morning! Honestly, I think the man smokes in his sleep. So I gave him another lecture and asked if I could get some whitewash and some stove black. And he was so nice—he gave me the key to the shop.'

She meant he was so flummoxed, Mike thought blankly. Anyone would be.

And William Harcourt... It couldn't have happened to a nicer man. Yellow ducks, eh? Mike's lips gave an involuntary twitch.

'So then I scrubbed and scrubbed. This place looked dingy but, in fact, it's just the smoke stains all over the stone walls from the fire stove. I'm sure Grandpa doesn't keep the vents open like he should and it's so bad for his health. I cleared everything out and whitewashed the walls, and I blacked the stove and then I hauled everything back in here—hasn't it made a difference?'

It certainly had. Mike could only stare.

'I need help to hang the curtains again,' she told him, not giving him time to comment. 'I washed them early and I was just going out to see if they were dry when I got sidetracked with Doris and the kids. I'll go and get them now. Isn't it lucky you came?'

And she flew out of the kitchen, leaving Mike staring after her.

She was like a whirlwind, a crazy, wonderful tornado that picked everything up and whirled it around and set it down...different.

And he didn't know how to stop himself whirling.

They worked steadily on. He wasn't allowed to protest. He simply obeyed orders and the experience was totally novel.

Mike was an undomesticated animal, but Tess didn't seem to notice. She had him hauling down the upstairs curtains, beating rugs over the clothesline, hauling sheets off beds and making them up with clean linen, and sweeping out rooms that hadn't been used for years. Strop followed behind, interested and nosing his way into everything.

'You and Henry are only going to use two bedrooms,' he protested. 'The place has five. Why do we have to clean them all out?'

His protest was met by scorn.

'If a job's worth doing, it's worth doing well,' she said piously. 'Didn't your mother teach you anything?'

And then she looked sideways at him as his face closed—and he knew she was busy adding two and two together and making heaven only knew what out of her thoughts. He didn't have the faintest idea what she was thinking.

He'd never met anyone like this woman in his life.

She called a halt at two. Miraculously the phone at Mike's hip hadn't sounded once. He almost wished it had.

Tess laid out fresh bread and cheese, and hauled a bottle of wine from her grandfather's cellar. She produced a hambone for Strop—how the hell had she guessed Strop might be here? Then she spread a rug out under the gums, settled herself down in the sunshine and she smiled up at him…

Then again, maybe he didn't want his phone to ring at all.

'Come on. You've earned this,' she ordered, patting the blanket.

'Where did you get all this from?'

'I begged the cheese from Louise's mom, the hambone came from the hospital kitchen and the baker was baking early this morning. I was his first customer. I told him I really hoped you might be sharing my lunch and he said he hoped so, too, and he said rye bread was your favourite.'

They'd be the talk of the town, Mike thought faintly. If Tess was breezing down the main street at dawn, chatting to solid citizens in their duck-covered pyjamas and discussing Mike's likes and dislikes in the bread department…

How *had* she known he would think of coming?

Miraculously, Tess was silent the whole time she ate. She lay stretched out like a lazy cat, soaking up the warmth and the fresh bread and cheese and the smell of the eucalyptus above them. He was left alone with his thoughts.

Not for long. Never for long with Tess around.

The bread and cheese finished, Tess disappeared inside the house and came back with two steaming mugs of coffee. She handed him one, settled down with hers and then hit him with both barrels.

'Tell me about your mother.'

'What....?'

'Louise says your dad lit out when you were tiny. She says your mother raised you alone and then, when you were sixteen, your mom died. How did she die?'

'Tess...'

'I know,' she said softly. 'It's none of my business. But tell me anyway.'

'Why?'

'Mike, I really want to know.'

He sighed and stirred and stretched out, lying on his back with his hands behind his head as he gazed up through the canopy of gum leaves. Why tell this girl? Why be here at all?

It seemed there was no choice.

'My mother died of a diabetic coma,' he said heavily, his voice sounding as if he'd been goaded. 'Her diabetes was unstable. She got an infection which ran out of control. One Saturday afternoon she just collapsed. In retrospect she needed intravenous antibiotics and she needed insulin. But she'd never let me touch her diabetic medical kit. She hated me even thinking she was ill, so I didn't know what to give her or how much—even if I'd known how to give an injection.'

His voice grew incredibly weary as he thought it through. How many times had he gone over and over what had happened? He was tired of it in his mind; infinitely tired, but he couldn't let it go.

'So…' Somehow he made himself continue. 'So there was no hospital here then and no nurses. There was just a doctor. Just a doctor who didn't come. Mum was in a coma when I found her, otherwise maybe she could have told me what to do. But there was no one.'

'You blame the doctor?'

'He should have come.'

'So you're going to be on call, twenty-four hours a day, seven days a week, for the rest of your life?'

'Something like that.' He grimaced, then shrugged and gave a rueful smile. 'No. I'm not that stupid. I know I'm not God. I pay locums once a year so I get a break.'

'Locums?'

'Two locums.'

'Two locums to provide the same service you provide?'

'That's right.'

'Because no other single doctor would be stupid enough to take on what you take on.' Tessa's voice was gentle, but insistent.

'That's your point of view.'

'Well…' She'd been sitting on the rug, staring down at him. Now she flopped backwards so she was lying full length beside him and she put her hands behind her head as well. She stared up into Mike's gum tree as if she was trying to see what he was seeing. By their side, Strop gnawed peacefully on, supremely content with his lot.

'It's just as well I've come, then,' she said decisively. 'You need me, Mike Llewellyn.'

'I—'

'Admit it,' she said, still staring upwards. 'You need another doctor.'

'If you stay, it'll mean I don't need to have so many holidays.'

'It'll mean you don't run yourself into the ground so much.' Tessa nodded decisively. She'd kicked her shoes off. Now she raised one bare foot and examined her toes, with the gum-tree canopy acting as a background for her painted toenails. It was as if she was admiring a work of art. Which, in fact, they were. 'So you admit it, Mike? You need me?'

'OK.' He stirred uneasily. She was too damned close for comfort—too damned close by far—and the sight of her bare toes… Hell, he'd never realised bare toes could be so sexy! 'I do need another doctor,' he said grudgingly. 'If you stay then I'll be grateful.'

'Oh, I'll stay.' She hauled herself up so she was supporting herself on her arms and staring straight down at him. Her face was now right in his line of sight—between him and his canopy. She was about four inches from his nose.

'And what about the rest of you, Dr Llewellyn?' she demanded.

'The rest?'

'The doctor part of you needs me as a doctor. Does the personal side of you need me as a woman?'

'Tess…'

'You're not saying there's no personal side?'

'Of course there's a personal side.'

'But not one that lets anything interfere with your medicine. Is that right?' she demanded. 'Because of what happened to your mother in the past you've blocked off your personal needs. And…' Her green eyes grew thoughtful. 'You think if you let yourself fall for me, I'll distract you.'

And then, as he stared up at her in baffled silence, Tessa's mouth creased into a smile. 'Hey, you might be right at that. Distraction sounds fun.' She put a teasing finger on his nose and her touch was electric. 'But I wouldn't distract you all that much, Dr Llewellyn. If duty calls I'll be right there beside you, beavering away like mad and being just as devoted a doctor as you. To suggest anything else is insulting.'

He stared up at her and she smiled straight back. Hell! Her curls tumbled down around her shoulders, just brushing his face. Her green eyes smiled down at him. Her face was so near…

Women weren't supposed to do this, he thought dazedly. Women weren't supposed to throw themselves at men.

This wasn't just a woman. This was Tessa.

'I wouldn't want to insult you,' he said faintly, and her smile grew.

'Now that's really wise.'

'Why is it wise?'

'Because I have friends in high places. Or low places. Insult me and I'll set Doris onto you.'

'Perish the thought.'

'She'd squash you to death in two seconds flat.'

'She'd do that on command?'

'She's a very amenable pig.' Tessa's voice softened and her nose lowered a notch or two. So there was about two inches clearance. 'Almost as well trained as your Strop. So…'

Mike could hardly breathe. His lungs were hurting. The sheer effort of not taking this girl in his arms was almost killing him.

But he didn't need to. Tessa had no need of assistance. She had things in hand here, and she knew very clearly what she intended.

'So just shut up, lie back and let me introduce you to a lady who intends to be the love of your life, Mike Llewellyn,' she whispered. 'And in case you hadn't guessed—that's me.'

Her nose descended a further two inches and Mike found himself being solidly kissed—and for the life of him he couldn't put up one skerrick of resistance. Somewhere inside him a weight was being lifted which had been almost too heavy to bear, and he hadn't known he was carrying it. He had sworn he'd never love, but he hadn't known what love was. He had sworn off commitment, but he hadn't known that commitment could be as sweet as this.

That a woman could feel like this in his arms... She felt as if she belonged right where she was—as if she were part of him. As if she were the completeness of his whole.

The last of his resistance crumbled. He held Tess to him and her body moulded itself to his in the soft autumn sunlight. At the touch of her body against his, Mike felt his vows slip away as if they'd never been.

Vows? What vows? They must have been unimportant things, made on the mistaken premise that he couldn't be committed to his medicine if he loved a woman.

He could be. This woman was his partner. He still could be committed, he told himself fiercely, because he had to be. Because, like it or not, he was wholly and wonderfully committed to the woman in his arms.

His Tessa.

CHAPTER NINE

THE next weeks passed like a dream, with Mike feeling as if a whole new world had opened up for him. Life was brighter, clearer—fantastic!

Everywhere he moved, there was Tessa.

Tessa's registration came through incredibly speedily. Her medical credentials, it seemed, were impeccable. The medical registration board thought so, and, on reflection, so did Mike.

The town was lucky to have her. Mike was lucky to have her—he just couldn't believe that it was happening. He felt like pinching himself to ensure its reality.

But Tess was real enough.

Mike watched her as she assisted him in rejoining Jason's torn Achilles tendon and he couldn't fault her anaesthetic skill.

He listened to her counsel Doreen, fiancée of Les Wade's nephew, Hugh. Doreen had drifted to Tess rather than Mike, wanting a female shoulder to cry on. Hugh was still in Melbourne where his uncle had started the long process of rehabilitation for his burns. Doreen and Hugh had postponed their wedding and Doreen was wavering between support of Hugh and fear that Hugh's guilt might prevent the marriage altogether.

Mike could only marvel at the way Tess stayed silent and let Doreen spill out her guilt and her anguish. The walls between the room Tess used as a surgery and the room Mike used as a file room needed to be soundproofed—long term there were all sorts of arrangements to be made if Tess was to stay—and Doreen's anguish was loud. Mike, sitting alone as he wrote up patient notes, could hear every word.

There were only gentle murmurs from Tess, though. Tess knew when to stay silent, as well as when to bounce with enthusiasm.

'Why don't you go to Melbourne and stay with Hugh?' she suggested softly, when Doreen had sobbed herself dry. 'Hugh will be feeling dreadful and that's where you should be. At his side.'

Doreen finally left, still sniffing into her handkerchief but comforted all the same. 'Are you sure it'd be OK?' she asked as Tess saw her to the door. 'I mean…our relatives all blame us for sleeping together in the first place. They think that's one reason why Les is in the mess he's in. If I go to Hugh now…'

'You follow your heart,' Tess suggested gently. 'If you think it's right, don't let anyone else stand in your way.'

Follow your heart…

Then Mike watched the way Tess helped her grandfather find his feet again. She spent hours assisting him to make his unsteady way along the hospital corridors, as if she had all the time in the world, and as if spending hour after hour watching an old man learn the skills of using a walking-frame was the most important thing she could possible be doing.

Henry thrived under her care, and Mike couldn't believe the speed of his recovery.

Tess got to know the locals. She introduced herself to every player of the Jancourt Football Club, and took the job of learning the rules of her new-found passion deadly seriously. To Mike's astonishment, she even started knitting a scarf in team colours.

'I think I'll do two matching ones,' she told him, clacking away at her knitting needles with the seriousness of a grandmother. 'Or maybe just one long one so we can wear an end each…'

And at night…

At night the farm lay empty. Tessa had cleaned it so she could stay there, and she still visited Doris and her babies each night and checked on the place, but late each night she returned to town and she took Mike into her arms—and she slept exactly where she wanted to be. With her Mike.

Even Strop seemed to approve. When Tess was there the dog left the bed to them, and in Tessa's body Mike found a peace he'd never thought to have.

Life had never been this good, Mike thought blissfully as he loved his woman. Mike had never known—never dreamed—it could be so good.

He held his love in his arms and he loved her—but only half of him believed in his good fortune. The other half of him knew he was living in a soap bubble.

'Hey, I'm not about to disappear,' Tess teased gently on the anniversary of their first two weeks together. 'I'm here for good.'

Mike didn't believe it, but he held her just the same.

In a town like Bellanor it was impossible to keep such a relationship a secret. After that first night—when Mike had emerged to Monday morning after a night spent with Tessa—he had been met with knowing looks and laughter.

'Bloody good thing too, Doc.' That was the general consensus. 'What took you so long?'

So long… A whole three days…

By the end of the two weeks the general approval was becoming laced with a stronger message.

'So, when are you going to make an honest woman of her, Doc? Get a mother for that crazy mutt of yours…?'

Marriage…

Mike had never thought of such a thing, but, once suggested, the idea stayed in his mind and wouldn't leave. He looked at it from all sides and knew his vow had definitely been broken already. He could hardly make it worse.

That night, Tess came with him when he did his weekly house call to Stan Harper. Stan was still suffering his chest pains and Mike was increasingly worried about him. His heart seemed strong and healthy, and yet Stan himself seemed to be almost fading.

'I'm just feeling bloody lousy, Doc,' Stan told him with an apologetic look at Tess. 'Pardon my French, miss.'

Tess had been sitting at ease at Stan's kitchen table while Mike listened to Stan's chest, and her face was sympathetic. 'I don't understand Australian swear words,' Tess lied. 'I'm trying to get Mike to teach them to me but he likes me unspoiled. I know ''damn'' means more than just a big puddle of water, but do you think he'll explain? No way!'

Stan chuckled and his misery lifted for a little while—but only for a little while.

'I'd like you to come into hospital for a few days,' Mike suggested as Stan hauled down his sweater. 'Stan, there doesn't seem anything wrong with your heart and the last three electrocardiographs have been normal, but if you're still having the pain…well, something's going on. Let's have you in and do a full check-up.'

But Stan would have none of it.

'Nope. I'm staying here. But you'll come again next Saturday?' His voice was anxious and Mike knew just how lonely the old man was.

'Tell you what,' Mike suggested. 'How about if I get the district nurse to call? I'll still come next week, but she'll come every other day as well. Just until we're sure everything's right.'

But Stan wasn't having that either. 'I don't want a fuss,' he said definitely. He sighed. 'Sometimes…well, yeah, I get chest pain and, yeah, I'm miserable but it's nothing that having Cathy back wouldn't fix.' He sighed again and looked closely from Mike to Tess. 'But look at the pair of you. Here's me fretting about myself when I should be saying how glad I am to see you finally wrapped around a woman's little finger, young Mike. You're smelling of April and May if ever anyone was. So when are you two going to tie the knot?'

Tess blushed and Mike shook his head.

'That's for us to know and you to guess,' he told Stan firmly—but the thought of what lay ahead was warm inside him. He glanced sideways at Tess and smiled—and she smiled straight back.

'Don't hang around too much, then,' Stan begged. 'It's too bloody important. You grab her while she's here. And hold on for dear life.'

The conversation in the Aston Martin on the way home was strained. Mike was trying to think about Stan, when all he wanted was to concentrate on Tess. They'd left Strop snoozing under Henry's bed for the afternoon, and it was lovely to be able to see Tessa instead of liver and white spots whenever he glanced sideways, but the sight of Tess—and Tess's leggings—wasn't helping his concentration.

'I'm still worried about Stan,' he told her stiffly.

'Mmm.' Tess pulled her knees up to her chin and hugged them. She was wearing black leggings and a vast purple sweater that covered her from her knees right up. She looked smashing.

'I don't think he's eating,' she said.

'Why do you think that?'

'Well, when we went there last week, I prowled,' she told him. 'When you had Stan in the bedroom, giving him the complete once-over, I poked my nose into his kitchen cupboards and just had a look at things—like the level of cereal in his cornflakes packet and what groceries there were and where they were. And tonight—when Stan walked us out to the car and I dived back inside because I'd left my bag—I had a fast look again and nearly everything's exactly the same. He hasn't touched his cornflakes. There's exactly the same number of eggs in the fridge as last week and when I picked one up and shook it, it sort of rattled—you know how really old eggs do? I reckon he's eaten a few bowls of tinned tomato soup, and not a lot else. Even the packet of bread in the freezer is the same one as last week. I ripped a little edge off the packet last week so I'd know it—and it's the same packet, only about six slices down.'

'You're a regular Sherlock Holmes.'

'I am,' she said smugly, but her smile faded. 'Do you agree?'

'It fits,' Mike said slowly. 'That's one of the reasons I'd like to admit him to hospital. He's losing a lot of weight.'

'He's missing his Cathy so much.'

'Yeah,' Mike said grimly. 'Love's like that. Once it hits, you can't get over it.'

'It's a problem,' Tess agreed, with a sideways glance at her love.

Silence. There seemed nothing else to say. The sleek Aston Martin ate up the miles between Jancourt and Bellanor and the silence stretched on and on.

Mike cast his own sideways glance. Tess was now looking straight ahead, peacefully contemplating the evening sky, and he came to an instant decision. This was impossible. He wanted her so much… Taking her in his arms each night, it was suddenly no longer enough.

'Marry me, Tess,' he said suddenly—urgently—and then held his breath.

'Marry you?'

'That's what I said.'

Tess closed her eyes. He hesitated, and then pulled the car off the road so they were facing down the valley to the town below. A bellbird was calling from the bushland outside the car, high and sweet and lovely.

And Tess sat silent for longer than he had dreamed possible.

'Tess?'

Surely there was only one answer here. Dear God, he loved her, and Henry had said she wanted marriage. She must love him.

But finally Tess opened her eyes, and as she did he knew what the answer was going to be. She turned to him and shook her head so her flaming curls flew free and her eyes were bleak.

'I love you, Mike,' she whispered. 'But I'm not going to marry you. Not yet.'

He moistened lips that were suddenly dry. His eyes didn't leave her face.

'May I ask why not?'

She tilted her chin with that look of defiance and pride he'd first seen in her—a look he'd come to know and love.

'Because you're asking me to marry you against your better judgement, and that's asking for trouble.'

'What do you mean?'

'I mean you think you're letting your mother down. By loving me, you've broken your vow. You'd marry me, and then you'd wait for the time when disaster happens. You know it'll happen some time, and you're right. Try as I may, if you marry me then some time in the future I'll interfere with your medicine. Sure, I'll help. Sure, I'll be beside you and medicine here will be better because of me, but when I finally get in your way I doubt it'll count on my part. You'll hate yourself. And you may well hate me.'

'You won't interfere with my medicine,' he said calmly,

surely. 'And there's no way I can end up by hating you. Tess, I've thought this through.'

'No, you haven't. Not properly.' Tess gave a lopsided grin and a shaky laugh. 'Mike, life will interfere with your medicine. All sorts of things can happen. A tree could fall on your head and you won't be effective as a doctor because you're squashed flat. You'd forgive the tree—or you would if you weren't squashed—because you haven't made any vows about never going near trees, but if I alter your life plan one bit and something goes awry because of it, you won't forgive me. Because when I interfere with your medicine you'll think it's because you broke your vow.'

She took a deep breath. 'I love you, Mike, but I want more than that—and I'm prepared to wait.'

Mike stared straight ahead through the windscreen, trying to sort out her words. Dear God… He was trying to pretend she wasn't saying exactly what he knew already—what he knew was the truth.

'This is stupid,' he said slowly.

'It might be stupid but it's how it is,' she told him, and he knew she wouldn't budge from her position. He'd been thinking things through, but so had Tess. He was prepared to risk problems because of his vow. What he hadn't counted on was that Tess wasn't.

She had it all figured out.

'Mike, I love you,' she repeated softly. 'And I'm prepared to hang in for the long haul here. But I want this disaster to happen before you totally commit yourself to me. I want you to see what loving me is all about—that it means letting life run its course side by side.'

'That's what I want.'

'No, you don't. Not yet.' Tess took a deep breath. 'Look, Mike, let's leave it. Believe it or not, I know what I'm doing here. I want you so much it hurts, but I'm not letting you make any more vows until you've come to terms with the last one you made. Until you let it go and accept that you can live with its release.'

She took his face in her hands and she kissed him gently on the lips. 'And you don't see what I mean yet, but I do. You need to wait. We both need to wait, Mike, to see what life throws at us. But no weddings. Just love... And let's just see if that's enough.'

Tess wouldn't budge from that position, and in the end he accepted it. He had no choice. It was crazy, he thought. She was wrong.

Oh, she wasn't wrong in that she thought he'd blame himself if he was distracted. What she didn't see was that he needn't be. With Tess as another doctor, surely there need never be a time when she'd stand in his way.

Meanwhile, though...life was still infinitely sweet. He and Tess worked side by side. The workload in the valley was magically halved. He had time to raise his head from work, and whenever he raised his head Tess was there, ready and willing to slip into his arms.

With his granddaughter as his chief medical specialist, Henry Westcott improved beyond any expectations. Five weeks from the time they'd found him, Tess and Mike prepared to take the old man home.

'I'll need to stay on the farm from now on,' Tess told Mike seriously on the Friday night before Henry was due for discharge. This would have to be their last night together. Both of them knew the difficulties now. The farm was too far from the hospital for Mike to be on call, even if he wished to stay with Tess.

He didn't. Even though Mike's body screamed its need for Tess, Mike knew Henry well enough to know that Tess sleeping unwed with Mike in Henry's house would upset the old man enormously.

But Tess was right. She had to stay.

'So we need to marry.' Mike smoothed the curls away from Tessa's face and kissed her deeply on the lips. 'Soon. Strop's going to miss you, and I'll miss you worse. Marry me.'

'Nope.'

'Nope?'

'Nope. You haven't had your disaster yet.'

'I'm not intending to have a disaster.'

'It'll happen. I'll tell you what, though.' She kissed him back, feather kisses that started on the tip of his nose, descended to his throat and kept on going. 'If you haven't had your disaster by the time I'm fifty, I'll marry you regardless.'

'Gee, thanks.'

'Don't you want to marry me when I'm fifty?'

Mike groaned. Her kisses were brushing his naked skin, down across his chest. Down…down…

'I may not live until you're fifty. I may not live another ten minutes. Tess…'

'It's a perfectly good offer. Take it or leave it.'

'Tess…'

'I'm serious.' She stopped kissing him for long enough to rise and brush the hair back from his eyes and meet his look with all gravity. 'Mike, it'll happen. I know it will. Let's just take this one day at a time and go from there.'

So on Saturday afternoon they borrowed the hospital car and Tess and Mike and Strop took Henry home, with Tess and Mike trying hard to act as though they were friends and not lovers. It didn't quite come off, but if Henry knew better he didn't let on. His joy at being home—at seeing Doris and her babies, and greeting his goats and sitting in his own armchair before the kitchen fire—was too great to let Mike's occasional stiffness mar it.

He sat and gazed around at their handiwork in delight.

'It's a bloody wonder,' he told her. 'Eh, Tess, girl...' His voice broke in rough emotion and Mike found himself feeling almost as choked up as Henry.

He had to leave. He'd had fallen into the habit of dropping in to see Stan Harper every Saturday evening so now he helped check out Henry's use of the walking-frame and his ability to get from the bathroom to the bedroom and back to the kitchen, and then it was time to go.

'Tess will take good care of you, sir,' he told Henry. 'And the district nurse will drop in on a daily basis.'

That was what they'd arranged. Also Matt, Jacob Jeffries's eldest lad, was coming each weekday morning—ostensibly to do some work on the fences around the house but in reality to keep a quiet eye on Henry for the first few weeks of his convalescence. That meant Tess could keep her morning clinic going and, as Henry grew stronger, she could take on more.

'You're not staying now?' Henry demanded, pulling himself out of his pleasurable haze to realise what Mike intended. 'Hell, you have to stay, boy. I asked Tess especially to cater for all of us. She's cooking a roast.'

'I am, too,' Tess said proudly. 'Roast pork.'

Mike's eyebrows hit his hair. Pork? Surely he'd still counted eight babies.

'You're kidding!'

Tessa's eyes crinkled in laughter at his tone. 'Don't even think it,' she told him. 'Perish the thought. This is a nice anonymous leg of pork bought from a nice anonymous supermarket. Donated, I'm sure, by a nice anonymous pig. I brought it in at dead of night so Doris wouldn't see, and I swear I'll bury the remains at dead of night, too.'

'Very wise.'

'So you will stay?' Tess grinned down at her grandfather and then back to him. 'I've bought a can of dog food for

Strop, and for us I have everything Grandpa ordered. Apple sauce. Butternut pumpkin. Roast potatoes and fresh peas, with lemon meringue pie to follow…'

'Lemon meringue pie…' Both men were now staring at her, their faces reflecting disbelief, and Strop was looking just plain hopeful. Bother the dog food!

'Hey, I'm not just a pretty face.' And then Tess relented and chuckled. 'Well, to be honest, Mrs Thompson made the pie for me, but the rest is mine. Do stay, Mike. We'd both like you to.'

He hesitated, but he was lost. Lemon meringue pie… Lemon meringue pie and Tessa… And Strop would break his heart if he hauled him away from these smells.

'Stan only needs a social visit,' he said slowly. 'I guess I can drop in tomorrow.'

He couldn't.

At eleven the next morning he finally arrived at Stan Harper's farm—and Stan was dead.

'It must have been a massive infarct,' Tessa said softly. It was Monday morning. She stood back from the autopsy table and looked across at Mike. She'd insisted on doing this. There was no way she was letting him do the autopsy on his own. 'There's no doubt,' she told him now.

'No.'

'Time of death, late on Saturday night?'

'How about late afternoon Saturday,' he said heavily, and Tess winced.

'No. There's no way we can say that.'

'There's no way we can say it was definitely later.'

'OK.' Tess crossed to the sink and started washing, watching him out of the corner of her eye. 'I'll accept that. It might have happened late Saturday afternoon.'

'When I should have been there.'

'By the look of this damage, there's no way you could

have helped, even if you had been there,' she told him. 'The artery's completely blocked. You know as well as I do that this wasn't a minor, recoverable heart attack. If he'd been in the best-equipped hospital in the world, I doubt he'd have been saved.'

'But there were no signs… Apart from the pain, which we couldn't pinpoint. The electrocardiograph was normal. I tried to get him to go to Melbourne and see a specialist but he wouldn't.'

'That was his choice.' Tessa's voice was flat and devoid of emotion. Her eyes were calmly watchful.

'I should have insisted.'

'And he would have refused.'

'At least I should have been there.'

Here it was. The crux of the whole matter.

'Are you saying if you'd been there you might have saved him?'

'Yes. No. I don't know.' He turned his face away and stared sightlessly at the bare wall. 'Who can say? He'd run himself down. He wasn't eating. If I'd spent more time there…bullied him into eating…'

'Instead of spending time with me,' she said softly.

'That did have something to do with it.'

'The fact that I'm taking so much of your workload that you have more time than ever before has nothing to do with it? The fact that if I hadn't been here, sharing your work, you might never have had time to pay any social visits at all?'

But he wasn't listening. 'I should have been there on Saturday evening,' he said solidly. 'I shouldn't have stayed on with you and your grandfather. I knew Stan was expecting me.'

'He wasn't expecting you. You'd called when you could. It was only because I've been able to give you free time that you've been able to go at all.' Tess sighed.

'Mike, Stan may well have been dead already if you'd arrived on Saturday afternoon—or he might even have been fine and then died after you left. There's no sign of previous scarring here. Apart from the chest pain, which you couldn't pin down on examination, there was no sign of such a massive problem. This was an act of God, Mike. It has nothing to do with you.'

'I should have been there.'

Silence. Tess dried her hands and pulled off her lab coat. Then she crossed the floor and took his hands in hers. He stared sightlessly down at her, his heart bleak.

'Mike, is this our disaster?' she asked softly.

'What...?'

'Will you hold this against us?'

He didn't look at her. He couldn't.

'I should have been there,' he repeated dully. How could he say anything else? It was all he could think. He'd let Stan down. He'd broken his vow. He'd known this would happen.

'Do you really believe that if you didn't love me then Stan would still be alive?'

But he couldn't answer. His face was cold and bleak and hard, and it reflected how he felt.

'I don't know, Tess,' he said finally. 'I don't know. All I know is that—'

'That you want me to go away?'

He closed his eyes, and when he opened them he knew what he had to say.

'Yes, please,' he said.

Silence.

'I knew this would happen,' Tess said softly—finally—and the pain in her voice was clear for him to hear. 'Aren't you pleased now that you didn't make another vow? Aren't you pleased we're not married?'

She walked slowly out of the room and closed the door behind her.

CHAPTER TEN

WHAT followed was an interminable month when Mike tried to pick up the threads of his life where he'd left off.

There were two sides to his life, he decided. Pre-Tess and post-Tess.

Pre-Tess had been bleak and hard. Post-Tess was just impossible.

He worked on two levels. On the surface he was efficient and calm and under control, but underneath he was so churned up he was wondering just how on earth he could cope.

Maybe it would get better in time, he told himself over and over. Maybe he'd get used to Tessa around the place and he'd stop wanting her in his bed at night. Strop was back on his pillow, and that was all the company he could allow himself!

Maybe if he stopped seeing her every time he turned around it might solve his problems.

That wasn't going to happen. Tess was settling further into valley life every day she worked here. She soon carved herself out a routine, coming in to do clinics every morning and taking her share of house calls in the afternoons.

Often she took Henry with her on her house calls. They purchased a reliable little truck between them, and the sight of the old man and the flame-headed young lady doctor, beetling around the valley roads, soon became a familiar sight.

'I don't know how you managed without her,' Mike was told over and over, and only he knew that he'd managed a darn sight better without her than with her. He was tearing himself in two!

'We were fine by ourselves,' he told Strop, but Strop's big, mournful eyes looked more mournful than ever, and his tail didn't wag at all. He hadn't minded sharing his Mike with Tess—and Tess was a dab hand with a can opener.

Mike's pain couldn't go unnoticed, especially by Tessa.

'You're being a dope,' she told him bluntly, six weeks after Stan's death. It was eleven at night. She'd come in to see a patient she'd admitted to hospital that afternoon, and came past the kitchen door to find him cooking himself bacon and eggs again. 'You'll kill yourself on that diet, and you're still working too hard.' She stood in the doorway and glared. 'You know damn well I want more work, Mike Llewellyn. Give it to me.'

'You can't work full time and look after Henry.'

'Henry's getting better every day. He's almost independent now.' She hesitated and then walked all the way in, sitting down at the table while he cooked. 'But that doesn't mean I'm leaving, if that's what you're hoping. Mike, I'm not going away. If anything, I'm getting closer. Henry and I have decided to sell the farm.'

'Sell the farm!' That rattled him.

'We love it but we don't need sixty acres,' she told him. 'And, living out there, I'm too far from the hospital. It was Grandpa's idea. There's a great little place down by the river just half a mile from here. Grandpa's been to see it and he loves it.'

'But he loves his farm.'

'So do we both. But we love being together more. This way we can stay together. Just me and Grandpa and Doris the pig…'

'And the eight porky babies?' He couldn't help himself. Mike's eyes twinkled and Tess twinkled right back.

'Come out and see our babies some time. They're what you might call good-dooers. Even Doris is feeling the strain. We may keep little Mike—or rather big Mike—but that's about the limit.'

'I see.'

'Mike…'

'Yes?'

Tess hesitated and then sighed. 'You're still blaming me for Stan's death—right?'

'No. I'm blaming me.'

'That's worse.'

'It can't be helped,' he said stiffly. 'It's the way it is.'

'So you're intending to stay solitary for the rest of your life? And keeping on working just as hard as you can?'

'That's the plan.'

'Well, it's a really stupid plan,' she burst out. 'Just crazy. Do you think your mother would thank you for doing it? For grudging me every piece of work I can get my hands on and for turning your back on a really magnificent love life? What with me and Grandpa and Doris and Strop, who could ask for more? And for running yourself into the ground because you're so damned miserable you've stopped looking after yourself?'

'That's ridiculous.'

'No, it's not,' she snapped. 'You should be eating three solid meals a day, with a nice family routine. Like with me and Grandpa and our appendages. Even with a couple of kids.' Tess flushed and then managed a smile. 'Well, if Doris can have little Mikes, I don't see why I can't. And as for living on bacon and eggs…'

'I like bacon and eggs.' Mike flipped his egg out on top of his bacon and stared down at it. Then he shoved the whole plate away. Suddenly he didn't feel like anything at all.

And Tessa's voice suddenly lost its aggressiveness.

'You're OK, aren't you, Mike?' Her face creased in sudden concern. 'You're not sickening for something?'

'No.'

'So you're not dying of a broken heart?' Her words were flippant, but her face was still worried. 'Mike, are you losing weight?'

'No.'

'I reckon you are,' Tess said slowly. Her eyes narrowed as she checked him out. 'In fact, I'm sure you are. And don't tell me. You don't really feel like that eggs and bacon.'

The plate lay before them, untouched. Mike hauled it back before him and picked up his knife and fork. 'Yeah. I do. OK?'

'So eat.'

'I'll eat when you leave.'

'I'm not leaving until I see you eat.'

'Tess...'

'Mike, is there something really wrong here? There is, isn't there?' All of a sudden Tess looked really worried. 'Mike, tell me—'

'There's nothing wrong,' he said explosively. 'I've just got a bit of a belly ache. That's all.'

'And tonight's the first time you've had it?'

'Yes!'

'OK.' Tess held her hands up in mock surrender. 'I know when I'm not wanted. But if it really has been going on for longer... If there's something wrong...'

'There isn't.'

'If there is...and you won't talk to me about it...' Tess hesitated. 'Or even take a few days off and see someone in Melbourne... Well, a man would be fool—wouldn't he?'

There was nothing wrong.

Tess left. Mike abandoned his eggs and bacon and took

himself back to his apartment, but Tessa's words kept playing in his head. A man'd be a fool...

There's nothing wrong, he told himself harshly, blocking off the thought of a few faint worries. There was no need to talk to Tessa or anyone else about this. It was just a nagging gut ache, that was all, and it was caused by nervous tension. There. The diagnosis was easy. He'd got himself in an emotional state over a woman and it was physically taking its toll.

He just needed time to sort himself out, he figured. He needed to divorce himself from what he was feeling for Tessa and then he'd be fine. He took some antacid and managed to eat and hold down a dry piece of toast. Then he said goodnight to Strop and went to bed.

That was at midnight. By dawn he was sicker than he'd ever been in his life.

'Have you seen Dr Llewellyn?'

Tess had been in the hospital for a whole five minutes before she was hit by the question. It was Horrible Hannah, about to go off night duty. Tess met Bill Fetson, coming on duty, in the hall and Hannah met them both.

'Mrs Carter's drip packed up about an hour ago and I need orders,' the nurse told them. 'I rang Dr Llewellyn's apartment but he's not answering. He must have gone out on a call but he's not answering his mobile phone either.'

'Maybe he's out of range,' Bill said. Then he frowned. 'But he knows where the phone cuts out. If he's going to be out of range then he rings first and tells us where he can be contacted.'

'Maybe he doesn't think it as important any more,' Tess said. 'Now that I can be contacted, he has back-up.'

'He doesn't like us contacting you.' Hannah shrugged. 'But I guess that must be it. Or he's somewhere where the lines are down. That's quite a storm outside.'

It was. The wind had been rising all night and now it was screaming around the sides of the building in the full blast of the onset of winter. A storm like this would be bound to bring the odd telephone wire down. Tess frowned but forced herself relax.

'OK, let's not worry,' she said—but she was worrying. 'I'll check Mrs Carter for you.'

She did and she ended up doing a full round of Mike's patients. There must be an emergency to keep him away, they decided, but there was nothing they could do until he contacted the hospital.

Tess had a house call of her own. She should leave now, but instead she made her way back to the nurses' station. Hannah was still there, having decided she didn't want to walk home until the worst of the weather had abated, and so was Bill.

'So, where is he?' she asked, and Bill shook his head.

'Beats me.'

'Has anyone checked his apartment?'

'Hannah's rung him more than once and there's no answer,' Bill told her. 'And I had Hannah walk down and check while I rang—just in case there's a fault in the line. There's not. From this side of his door you can hear it ringing inside. Oh, and Strop's inside. You can hear him snuffling at the door. Mike must have decided to leave him indoors because of the weather. Mike has to be out.'

'Yes, but…' Tess hesitated, her face creasing in worry. 'It's just… Bill, last night Mike didn't look well. He was off his food.'

Bill stilled. They looked at each other for a long, long minute. Outside, the wind blew more fiercely.

'Bill, what are we waiting for?' Tess said at last, and in her heart there was suddenly a lurch of real fear. 'Let's check.'

Strop met them as they unlocked the door and he was

frantic with worry. He saw them inside and launched himself at the bathroom door, barking in a frenzy.

By the time they reached the bathroom they were expecting something bad, and they found it.

Mike was stretched out, unconscious, on the bathroom floor.

Mike surfaced to the Horrible Hannah.

For a long moment he couldn't figure out where he was. He lay absolutely still and let the room come into focus. It didn't completely. It spun, but as he stared upwards the spinning slowed.

And then Hannah was looking down at him.

'Oh, Dr Llewellyn. Oh, Mike!' There was no mistaking it. For the first time in his life, Mike heard real emotion in Hannah's voice. Joy. 'You're awake. Oh, don't you dare shut your eyes. I'm fetching Tess.'

Tess... Hannah was calling Tess *Tess*?

It was all too much to work out, and there seemed no need. He was so damned tired. He couldn't help it. Try as he may he couldn't obey Hannah's order. His eyes closed all by themselves, and he slept.

The next time he opened his eyes Tess was there. And she was crying.

He'd nearly died, and it took him days to figure out why he hadn't. Days while Strop lay as devoted watchdog under his bed and his body slowly recovered from its shock.

'You had a massive bleed from a duodenal ulcer,' Tess told him, in a voice that still shook. 'I've never seen so much blood. We put five units of plasma aboard before we started operating, and once we'd cross-matched we had donors coming in from all over the valley. We needed them all.'

Operating... That was another thing he couldn't work

out. Somehow he'd been operated on, and he'd been operated on here.

'You were operated on by me,' Tess said when he was finally well enough to ask the right questions. 'And don't ask me how I did it because I don't know and I never, ever want to do such a thing again. You're trained in general surgery but, apart from my basic medical training, I'm not.'

'So how...?'

But Tess shook her head, and her voice trembled. She reached out and took his hand in hers, and it wasn't just her voice that was trembling. 'Please, Mike, don't ask. I can't think about it.'

It was up to Bill to tell him, and it was two days after the operation before he was well enough to take it all in.

'It was a bloody miracle,' Bill growled, as he changed Mike's dressings with hands that were amazingly tender for such a big man. 'I'd written you off myself. As soon as I saw you on the floor and saw the blood...well, I was all for calling the undertaker. If it hadn't been for Tess, you'd be pushing up daisies by now.'

'So, what happened?'

'We couldn't evacuate you,' Bill told him. 'The weather was foul and no helicopter could get in, even if there had been enough time to get you to a major hospital or get a surgeon flown in here. Which there wasn't. And here you were, losing blood like a stuck pig. Tessa was pouring in plasma but it wasn't nearly enough. You were dying under her hands. So she said...she said she was going in.'

'But... How the hell...?'

'That's what we all said,' Bill said grimly. 'You've got no idea... There was me and Hannah and Louise and Tess and Strop—all standing around staring at each other like helpless dummies. We were pouring in blood but we were still losing you. And then Tess said we had nothing to lose so who was going to do the anaesthetic?

'And I just gaped at her—but Hannah said she'd have a go if Tess told her everything to do. Hannah's such a poke-nose—there's nothing she misses and she's been a theatre nurse in the city. So Tess took a deep breath and says great and not to worry because it might be the first time Hannah's given an anaesthetic but it's also the first time Tessa's ever been a surgeon. Which, you can imagine, made us feel a whole heap better...'

'Yeah?' Mike was trying hard to concentrate here. The pethidine was making him drift in and out of reality, but he was getting the gist of it. 'So...'

'So Tess rings Melbourne,' Bill said. 'You should have heard her. Bossy? You wouldn't believe it. She organised a phone link with two specialists, one for her and one for Hannah—one anaesthetist and one specialist surgeon. They link up. We use that teleconferencing line you put in, where we talk hands-free. I turn up the volume so both Hannah and Tess can talk and the two specialists can listen and throw in advice as needed.

'Maybe Tess could have advised Hannah on the anaesthetic—she did a bit and kept her eye on her—but she's got her hands full with what she's doing to you.'

Bill shook his head, and the tone of his voice indicated that what had happened was still unreal to him. 'We had every nurse in the place back in here,' he said. 'There were people taking blood donations and helping in the wards and in the theatre. Everybody wanted to help.' He gave a rueful grin.

'And for those who weren't needed and knew what was going on, Father Dan ran a special Mass. Tess said go right ahead, she needed every ounce of help she could get and she'd accept it from any direction she could. Oh, and Strop sat outside the kitchen door and howled.'

'But she did it,' Mike said faintly.

'Yeah. She did it. You know you arrested on the table?'

'You're kidding.'

'Nope. Hannah nearly died as well, she was so frightened, but Tess stayed calm. Stopped what she was doing—had me hold the clamps—and put on the electrodes. Jump-started you. Got the heartbeat going, reassured Hannah and then calmly went back to stitching the damned ulcer up. She did it like a professional, and the surgeon advising her told me afterwards that he doubted if he'd have stayed as calm as she was.'

And then Bill gave a rueful smile.

'Maybe she wasn't all that calm, though,' he said grimly. 'After it was all over and you'd opened your eyes and she'd seen you might make it…well, I went outside and she was throwing her guts up. Vomiting like it was she who'd had the ulcer and not you. You put her through the hoops, boyo, and that's the truth.'

'Hell.'

'It was all of that.' Bill's smile softened and he gripped Mike's hand. 'All of that and more. Its bloody good to have you back. But Tess…'

'Yeah?' It seemed there was something else on Bill's mind but he was having trouble saying it.

'Well…' Bill shrugged and then dived straight in. 'When I was helping her clean herself up she told me you won't marry her because she interferes with your medicine. Crying her eyes out when she said it. Of all the stupid things… She interferes with your medicine? Without her loving you… Without her worrying enough to practically kick your apartment door down, without her taking risks you wouldn't believe and laying her professional reputation on the line…way beyond the call of duty… Well, without Tessa, you'd be giving this community no medicine at all. Never again. You'd be one more statistic for the graveyard.'

* * *

'Tessa?'

'Mmm.'

White-coated and efficient, Tessa had breezed into his ward, Hannah behind her. She picked up his obs chart and beamed at what she saw. 'This is great,' she said. 'You know, we might start you on solids tomorrow.'

'No eggs and bacon, though.' Hannah grinned and Tessa smiled her agreement.

'You're right, Nurse. No eggs and bacon. We might try a little jelly and—'

'Tessa!'

'Sorry, Mike. Were you trying to say something?' Tessa raised her eyebrows and gave him her entire attention—just like a really polite general surgeon.

'Yes. Can we have a minute alone?'

'I'm afraid Hannah and I are really busy.' She smiled again. 'You understand we have the entire medical needs of the valley on our shoulders. We can't let our personal lives interfere.'

'Tessa!'

'Yes?' Once again that polite enquiry, though a twinkle lurked behind those green eyes.

'I need to ask you something.'

'Ask away.'

'Alone!'

'I'm sorry.' She smiled benignly. 'You, of all people, must know it's professionally unwise for a lady doctor to be alone with a male patient. Hannah's my chaperon.'

Hannah beamed. Goaded, Mike could only stare. Hannah had come right out of her shell. What she'd done had shed years of bitterness from her shoulders. The nurse was practically giggling.

'You don't need a chaperon,' he managed.

'Remind me to tell you what I need some day,' Tess said

gently. 'I think I have in the past, but you haven't listened. Now…is there anything I can do for you?'

'Yes.' He glowered. 'I want you to marry me.'

'Oh, is that all?' Her brow cleared, and the twinkle came back. Behind the laughter there was joy. 'I think we could organise that. Hannah, when you go back to the nurses' station, could you see if you could find a time in my diary…?'

'Tess—'

'We wouldn't want it to interrupt the medical needs of the community, now, would we?'

'Tess—'

'Must go,' she said airily, breezing out. 'But, of course, I'll marry you. Anything to oblige, Dr Llewellyn. Anything to keep my patients happy.'

It was two days before he could get a serious answer. For two days she either had Bill or Louise or Hannah at her side, and he was almost going crazy.

Finally he caught her. It was midnight. He'd been dozing, half-asleep, a state he'd been in constantly since his operation as his body started to recover. He heard the door open gently, the slit of light enlarged and he heard soft footsteps coming toward the bed.

Silence. He closed his eyes.

Whoever it was bent over him. He would recognise that smell anywhere. His hand came out and grasped her wrist before she had a chance to pull away.

'Nice,' he growled. 'Stay.'

'Mike…'

All of a sudden, Tessa's voice sounded really unsure. Mike's eyes widened. He brought his other hand up to grasp her other wrist, and he pulled her down closer.

'I've been wanting you so much.'

'I don't know why. You're not much use to me like you

are.' Tess managed a soft chuckle and motioned to the tubing around his bed. 'All wired up.'

'I don't want to make love to you.'

'No?'

'Well…' He smiled, and the warmth in the little room grew and grew. 'Well, not so much…not as much as I want to talk to you.'

'I've agreed to marry you,' she said primly. 'What else do you want?'

'I want to say I'm sorry.'

'Sorry…'

'For ever doubting you. For being so bloody stupid. For causing you one moment's pain.' Mike closed his eyes. Hell, he was still so weary, but he had to say this. He must! 'Tess, you are the loveliest…the most precious…the most wonderful woman I have ever met. I can't believe you love me but if you do…you'll have given me the most precious thing I ever could ask in life.

'I love you so much, Tess. I want you beside me, and I want you beside me for ever. I've had my share of disasters. I want your love before I face any more. From now on, any disasters that come, we'll face them together.'

'Mike…'

'Tess, marry me,' he whispered. 'Marry me and know I have no reservations. Marry me and know that I can't be a doctor without you. I can't be anything without you. You're half of my whole. Tess…'

'Oh, Mike…' And she knelt and buried her face in his shoulder, and her arms came around him, tubing and all.

'Mike, don't be silly.'

'I'm not silly. I'm asking—'

'And I've already answered,' she said steadily. 'I fell in love with you the moment I saw you and I'll love you for ever. Of course I'll marry you. Of course I'll marry you, my love. I intended to from the first and I intend to now.

To love you without stopping. You just get yourself better, and then we'll plan a wedding to die for. Or…' She thought about what she'd said, and that irrepressible grin twinkled out. 'Maybe we'd better say a wedding to live for. Because that's just what it's going to be.'

As weddings went, it was unusual to say the least.

Tess had announced where her wedding was to be held and the community had blinked. So had Mike, but she'd dragged him out there and held him close, and he'd seen what she'd seen.

And he blessed her for it.

Six weeks after Mike's operation he stood, clad in dinner suit, white carnation in his buttonhole, the sea breeze ruffling his hair and with an almost overwhelming happiness in his heart, and waited for his bride.

The headland where the wedding took place was one of the loveliest places in Bellanor, nestled between two mountains about three miles from town. The homestead here had long fallen into disrepair. The land was used for cattle agistment and nothing else. The bush had reclaimed the land on the bluff and it had taken a working party three days to clear enough room for the portable chairs and the vast marquee and the tiny altar.

There was normally nothing here. Just sea and bushland and native birds—and one solitary grave.

This was the headland where Mike's mother was buried. Her grave was covered with a mass of native orchids, almost an altar in itself, and it was here that Tess decreed she'd marry.

'Because we're going into this with our eyes wide open,' she told Mile solemnly. 'You're not breaking any vow. You're renewing it, with a difference.'

And so he was. He was renewing it, with joy thrown in for good measure. With Tess…

And here she was, pulling up in Harvey Begg's Volvo, with Henry climbing out to proudly take her arm. Henry hardly had the need for his walking-frame now, and there was no way he was using it to give his girl away. His old eyes beamed with happiness and pride.

Louise and Hannah fluttered forward, fast friends now with no trace of the Horrible Hannah of old. They adjusted Tessa's dress, a floating confection of white lace, cut low at the breast and flaring out in soft clouds to form a train behind. It wasn't entirely white. It had soft, fine red ribbons laced through the bodice, and on her feet she was wearing…

Mike blinked. She was wearing red stilettos—the red stilettos he'd fallen in love with the first time he'd seen them! The first time he'd seen her.

Tess. His lovely Tess. His gorgeous, crazy, wonderful bride! Her wonderous red hair was floating free, and he thought he'd never seen anything more beautiful in his life.

He glanced to the front row where Tessa's mother was sitting. She was a firebrand just like her daughter, and she was sitting serenely with a dog lead in her hand. The lead was attached to a gleaming, groomed and handsome Strop, resplendent in crimson bow.

Strop was looking so mournful he was almost smiling.

Of course he was smiling. This was so right. All the pieces of Mike's jumbled life were fitting together, and his Tessa was walking steadily toward him.

Tessa… His bride…

And her eyes were loving him.

There were no doubts in Mike's heart now. There were no doubts at all. This was right. This was his fate. This was where he was meant to be.

Everything seemed to hush as Mike and Tessa made their marriage vows.

And it was right for this marriage to take place here.

Drifting around them was the spirit of times past—the echoes of the love Mike had once had here with his mother. It was an echo that would now resound down the generations, with Mike's and Tessa's children, and with their children's children, and beyond.

There was no judgement here. There was only love. There was love and there was happiness, and there was all the hope in the world for a future of joy.

MILLS & BOON®

Makes any time special

Enjoy a romantic novel from Mills & Boon®

Presents...™ Enchanted™ Temptation®

Historical Romance™ Medical Romance™